Captain Harry,
The Son Of Di Beach
And
The Mystery Of
Crazy Chester

Many thanks and much love,
not just now but always,
to my family and friends.

And a special thank you
to all my Facebook islanders.

If you would like to visit
di Facebook island, go to
www.facebook.com/livelikeajimmybuffettsong

Chapter One

Arr.

No, that's not quite right, either.

Yes, I am a pirate, late or not, and I've done my fair share of plundering. But that's not who I am. When opportunity knocks I might go answer if I'm feeling energetic enough, but I don't go chasing after it with shady folks sporting eye patches and peg legs. I have been known to partner up with them, however, but they move too slow these days to go chasing after much of anything with me.

My wooden appendaged accomplice with no depth perception in question's name was, and is, the fisherman. Or fisherman, if you're talking to him face to face. We don't say, *"How's it going today, the fisherman?"* like a bunch of idiots. But if you ask him who he is, he's going to tell you he's the fisherman, every time. Or even more accurately, di fisherman.

No one knows what his real name is, or if he ever even had one. Or for that matter, why he's called the fisherman. Yeah, he loves to fish. So do most of the folks around here, including me, but none of us have changed our monikers yet. And there's no one called the farmer, the mechanic, the fornicator, or the drinker, either. We do have a Coconut Man but he doesn't have a the, so I don't think he counts. That makes the fisherman one of a kind, which I could have told you in the first place.

But I suppose you want to hear more about me, since it's my name written in the title. Well, I'm not gonna sit here and question your taste, even though it obviously deserves scrutinizing. For starters, I'm in that forty-ish range where people, especially men, tend to go a little crazy. I guess I was in a hurry, though, because I went off the deep end a few years early; then again, I tend to think I was more or less pushed off that cliff, or at least nudged towards it.

I lived in one of those big cities in the northern part of the U.S. of America. Which one doesn't really matter; when you get down to it, those big cities are all the same, it's just their sports teams have different names. I owned a chain of dry cleaning stores throughout the area, and had a wife and two sons, none of whom really seemed to like me all that much (well, maybe the stores did, since I spent most of my time with them). I'm not going to go any further into what went wrong with my family life; it doesn't matter now. My fault, their fault, life's fault, it's over now. Sometimes people are just plain better off without one another.

Anyway, among all the things that weren't working particularly well for me at the time, was that for some reason my stores kept getting robbed, and it was beginning to piss me off to no end. I mean, who robs a dry cleaning store? Usually I wasn't there when it happened, since I couldn't be in five places at once. But then one rainy afternoon a guy came in and waved a gun at me and my clerk, and demanded I give him my money. And all I can say is, I played linebacker in college, and when I looked at him, all I saw was a skinny little quarterback, and a cocky one at that. So I did a hurdle over the counter and tackled him (and pulled a muscle in my calf in the process, which ended up being the least of my problems). I must have surprised him, because he didn't shoot me right away; he waited until we were lying on the ground in a heap for that. I took it in the same calf muscle I'd just pulled and did some sort of a yowl and rolled off him, and he ran out of the store, probably in search of establishments with less hostile and stupid owners.

Everything kind of went downhill for me after that. There wasn't much I felt like doing, except limping around and moping. I realized later that I wasn't at all happy even before the shooting, and that it was just the hole through the icing on my donut. Even my one great joy in life, my flying, didn't do it for me anymore. Maybe because when I took off into the sky I was somewhere and someone else for a while, but when I came back down to Earth, it was always to the same old me and place.

And then one day, I didn't. Come back, that is. My wife and kids were going to see her parents for the weekend, and I wasn't invited (yeah, things were that bad, and I don't blame here; I didn't want to be with me either). I got into my plane with a flight plan to take me to another nearby big city, intending to stay the night there and see and do the same old crap but in a different location, as if that was going to perk me up. But things didn't end up working out that way.

Instead, like Forrest Gump, I just kept going. And going and going, until I hit the ocean down in Miami. But unlike Forrest, I didn't turn around and go the other way when I came to the water. I got out of my little aero plane, went inside the airport, and booked passage on a much bigger flier into the Caribbean. I did call my ex-wife and let her know, though, just before boarding call. And I say ex-wife because I knew at the time that that's what she was going to be when I dialed the phone. She probably actually was destined for it even before that, but that was when I truly realized it. My life as I knew it was over, and I was going off in search of a different one I liked better.

It took quite a few weeks, but I found it on the island of Paradiso Shores; or maybe it found me. I'd been looking for something to do, some store, hotel, or bar to buy and improve, and to fill with tourists. And yeah, I was still looking to make money at the time, so I guess I had a few lingering strands of my old ways. But what I ended up with instead was nothing close to what I'd had in mind, even if six years later I couldn't be happier with the way things turned out.

To tell you I won my half of the Rumwrecked Bar from the fisherman in a poker game would be too much of a cliche, so I won't. It'd be a lie anyway, since I won it playing dominoes. And I didn't win half of it, I won all of it; I just felt guilty the next morning about taking an old man's livelihood away from him. Not enough to give him all of it back, mind you, but enough to give him forty-nine percent of it, at least. And he was lucky to get that, since if I would have known he was trying to get rid of it to some unsuspecting schmuck like me, I just would have kept the whole damned thing for myself.

He's never admitted it to me, but I'm pretty sure the fisherman wanted out, although ending up only half out probably suited him even better. Like I said, he was getting old, and running even as laid back a paced place as the Rumwreck was getting to be too much. It's the only way to explain my beating him at dominoes three straight games that night. I found out later he was a local legend at rolling those bones, which was how he had gotten the bar in the first place. I know I haven't seen him lose more than a couple of games back to back since, and against a lot better players than me. Hell, except for the turistas, they're all better than I was at the time, considering I hadn't played since I was nine. And yeah, it is harder being good at it than it looks.

I've upped my game a bit since though, and now at least I can hold my own. Just like the fisherman can hold his part of the bar, too; the end he sits at all day, anyway. Oh he'll limp off to the back now and then to get another bottle of Captain Billy's Black Dog Rum, bitching all the way of course, if I plead hard enough. But unless he spots a pretty senorita at a table down by the water to greet, in which case he moves faster with that timber for a leg he has than Usain Bolt, he's pretty much a barnacle on a bar stool. But that's okay; it wouldn't be the Rumwreck without him.

As for the Rumwreck Bar itself, it has one of those names that's constantly in flux. The big wooden sign overhead reads, *"The Rumwrecked Bar"*, but the one on the dock says simply, *"The Rumwreck"*. Our tee-shirts say, *"I got wrecked at the Rumwreck"*, but the one of a kind, hand blown shot glasses we sell have *"Rumwrecked"* painted on them. And then there's the bulk of the people around here, who simply call it *"The Wreck"*.

I guess a name is just a name and it doesn't really matter, and since we don't have a Facebook page we don't have to settle on just one. Advertising isn't exactly an ongoing concern here on Paradiso Shores, so we can call ourselves whatever we want in any given moment. In fact, being exact isn't exactly a concern either; around here, just being is mostly what matters. That and the aforementioned fishing, of course.

But I'm starting to ramble now. And while that may be an acceptable practice in the islands, it's not nearly as appealing on the written page. The only reason I'm even doing this is because it seems like jotting down your adventures is the kind of thing displaced men in the Caribbean sporting sweat stained Panamanian hats like me do. Although I don't know if there's enough of me to go around for more than one story. But I do know that if I'm going to keep writing I'm going to have to get myself a typewriter, since my hand is getting mighty cramped holding this pencil. And no, I'm not getting a laptop; the only laptop I'll ever own now is the one I already have, and its main function is as a bench for a wench.

So to quickly finish up my life story until now, I went back home, got a quick but painful divorce, found someone else to run my stores and set it up so that my wife and sons got most of the money, and that I'd get just enough to do what little I wanted to do. Then I sold my plane, took some lessons, and bought a new one with floats. And finally, I moved myself and what little belongings I felt mattered down to this backwards tropical island in the middle of nowhere.

Soon after, I got tired of sleeping in a hammock and bought a boat, the Anchored Away, and parked it at the end of one of the docks in front of this wreck of a bar I got tricked into owning half of. And six or so years later, I'm still here, wondering what the hell went so wrong and right with my life.

I'm your typical expatriated American, I guess, even though I hate the term. Because I still love the good old U S of A, and I'm as patriotic about it as the next guy. Maybe even more so, now that I'm not there dealing with all its day to day political and corporate run bullshit; it makes it a lot easier to feel all warm and fuzzy about Uncle Sam when you're in a long distance relationship with him. And I am still a citizen, and still consider myself to be an American; I just don't happen to live there anymore, and we're both the better off for it. I know I am, anyway.

Hopefully I've at least managed to lay out some kind of groundwork for whatever the hell it is I'm going to write about next, and that whoever reads this will have some idea at this point about how I came to be where I am. Probably not, and I'll no doubt have to explain it further as I go along. Other than that, I'll just say that my name is Harry. Not *the* Harry like *the* fisherman, but just plain Harry. Although a lot of people around here call me Captain Harry for some reason I've never fathomed out. I'll answer to it, too; I've been called a lot worse, and probably will be again.

Like when one of the islanders calls me a son of di beach. I don't think I'll ever know for sure if they're referring to my transmogrification into a beach bum or if they're making a statement on my temperament. I'm guessing it's a bit of both, and that's fine by me too, since either way it's the truth.

Cuz I am Captain Harry, the son of di beach.

Chapter Two

"I'm tellin' you mon; you cannot beat a Shimano reel for mahi-mahi," said Keyon.

"Are ya crazy? Anyone with half a brain knows an Okuma wins hands down," snorted Kian. "Of course, dat leaves you out."

"Is dat a fact? Den who was it again dat caught di twenty-six pounder? Because my memory be gettin' a little fuzzy. Was it you?" said Keyon.

"One big fish! One! And dat was seven months ago. And me tink di scaly one was mentally impaired; a lot like you," retorted Kian.

"You just jealous because all di fish you catch be smaller den di bait," said Keyon. "Di only reason dey can even get on di hook is because dey have a mouth as big as yours."

"And if di fish you catch had a mouth as big as you, dey could swallow di whole boat!" said Kian.

It was late morning debate hour by the sea, starring Keyon and Kian. It took place pretty much every day at the Rumwreck, right on schedule, over island coffee, fruit, and Caribbean bread. It didn't matter what it was concerning; the two twin brothers would find something to bicker about. They could even argue over how wet water was, and I'm not exaggerating, since I'd seen them do it round about every rainy season.

"Ding!" I said finally, officially ending their dispute (which was my job as moderator), at least for this morning. "This one goes to Kian."

"You always pick Kian," complained Keyon. I didn't know how they knew which one of them I meant, since their names sounded identical to me and I pronounced them that way, but they always did.

"No, he doesn't," said Kian.

"Yes, he does," said Keyon. "You just can't remember, because you be too busy day dreaming about goats."

"Alright, you two, you know the rules; only one argument per morning, so make peace already before I sic the fisherman on ya," I said. I took a sip of coffee, then watched as Starch flopped onto his back and went stiff.

"Sorry, Captain," said Kian. "We going fishing later, Keyon?"

"Sure ting, mon," said Keyon. "I'll bring di beer."

"Den I got di grub," said Kian.

And like most brothers, when the argument was over, they went back to being best friends. Or maybe that wasn't how most brothers were; I'd never had one, so I could only go by the two of them. But it was how I thought brothers should be, anyway.

"Where is the fisherman, anyway?" I asked, as Starch continued to lie unmoving on the table.

"He took his boat over to di island to pick up some rum," said Maggie May, from behind her month old copy of the Detroit Free Press. Maggie May was our expatriated (and she *was* expatriated, having absolutely no time or patience for America anymore) local general store owner, slash mechanic, slash glass blower from Detroit who hadn't been named after the song. Or so she claimed, anyway. "He said you were getting low on Gold."

"I wonder what the hell got into him?" I said, finally giving in and offering Starch a piece of papaya bread before he decided to stay permanently dead. He happily accepted it, hopping onto his feet and coming back to life with a squawk, then grabbing the bread greedily with his beak as my fingers made yet another narrow escape. I watched him devour it, then said, "I told the fisherman not to pilot that little dinghy of his across the ocean anymore; he and it are getting too damned old."

"He mentioned something about that as well; now, how did he put it?" said Maggie May, cocking her head sideways in mock thought. "Oh yeah; he said to tell you he's been sailing since before your daddy fell in love with di mule and had you, and to shut di hell up, and to mind your own damned business before he teaches you a lesson once and for all."

"So I take it he was in a good mood today, then?" I said.

"Never better," said Maggie, before going back to her paper.

I was pretty sure we weren't that low on any of our rums yet; we'd have to have sold some lately in the first place, and Paradiso Shores wasn't exactly an island bustling with tourons at the moment. Not that it ever was, mind you; we were pretty much uncharted on most rubberneck maps, which suited most of us just fine. The only reason I even bothered keeping a stock of a couple of cases of each of the different Island Rum Company rums was for my own variety sake, and in case an impromptu island party broke out, which was far more likely to happen than a big boatload of the aforementioned tourists arriving out of the blue. The real excuse for the fisherman to have gone to di island this morning was probably to visit someone like the Innkeeper, Jolly Mon, or Crazy Chester, for a fishing or general bullshit session. And to chalk it all up to company business on our metaphysical time sheets.

It wasn't like we officially kept track of such things since no one really got paid anyway, but it

17

meant the next time I started bitching at him for not doing anything around here because he started bitching at me about having too much to do, he could point out that he'd just gone all the way to di island to get more rum. *Just* being any time in the last three months, of course. But it all worked out in the end; the fisherman would have his visit and mock work, and I'd have a goodly number of hours of not having to hear him complain about how I didn't have a clue what I was doing, and how I was running his place into the ground. So it was all good unless he drowned or got eaten by sharks, or both, which could put a real damper on my, and his, day.

It would have been hard, in my own humble opinion, to run the Rumwreck into the ground or into much of anything else; it just sort of sat anchored there taking up beach space, looking like it had washed up on shore years ago and decided to stay. The building itself was a simple one story structure with a dilapidated thatched roof over the storeroom and bar, which stubbornly managed to stay standing in every high island wind only because it was so experienced at always being about to fall down.

There was an overhang just wide enough for about a dozen people and six bar stools to huddle under out of the sun or afternoon rain, and a nearby crusty canvas hanging from dried out wooden poles provided shade from the same elements for a few more. Other than that, a couple of hammocks and a handful of formerly brightly painted picnic tables were scattered around the sand under the sun and on down to the beach where a rock fire pit resided. All in all, there wasn't a whole lot of anything for me or anyone else to ruin.

But while it wouldn't be considered much more than an eyesore in every TGIF corporate guru's mind, the Wreck was still heaven on Earth to me. Better than that, in fact; it was more like the Garden of Eden, and I'd stomp on, then skin and eat the serpent's ass that tried to get me thrown out of it. And any Eve's that dropped by could hawk apples at me all day if they wanted, pushier than any timeshare salesman; I had my papayas, pineapples, pomegranates, and mangoes. Which evidently had been missing from Eden in the first place, if Adam was tempted enough by one wormy apple to risk godly lighting bolts and eviction from paradise.

"I'm not gonna know what to do with myself without the fisherman to boss me around," I said.

"Maybe you could finally fix the roof over the bar," suggested Maggie.

I looked over and examined it, sitting there perched on the building like a giant hula skirt that had landed there and lost its hula. "I don't think I dare touch it," I said. "It's been like that for at least six years, and if I move even one straw, I might destroy what little structural integrity it has left."

"It is a mystery what keeps it up," said Maggie, adjusting the stained and beaten Red Wings cap I'd sent away for her years ago.

"Too lazy to fall down, I tink," said Kian.

"Are you still here, Kian?" I said. "If you don't get moving and go have some fun, I'm gonna change my mind and put you to work with Keyon; if he ever gets up and actually does any work himself. Like opening the bar, which he's supposed to before the rush doesn't hit us."

"I'm out of here den," said Kian, standing up quickly. "I'll see you later today, my brother." And he disappeared around the side of the bar, heading through the scattering of palm trees towards the dirt road.

Keyon continued to sit staring out into the distance, firmly engrossed in doing nothing.

"I thought I just told you to get to work," I said to him. "Or was my hint a little too subtle for you again?"

"Well, mon; you did say *if* I ever do any work, so I figured you meant it was optional today," Keyon said with a grin, testing me as usual.

"Then how about this; move your ass...now!" I growled at him.

"Dat's di son of di beach we all know and love," Keyon said happily, and he slowly got up and shuffled towards the bar, satisfied now that he'd gotten me riled up yet again.

"I guess that just leaves you and me, Maggie," I said. "Any ideas?"

Starch, my little Amazon Parrot, took that moment to squawk and fly off the table and up into a nearby tree, evidently irritated at being left out of the group.

"We could always have sex, if you've got nothing better to do," said Maggie May, without looking up from her paper.

I gave her suggestion its due moment of thought, then said, "Naw; it's getting too warm. I already took my cold shower for the day, and I don't want to get all sweaty again and have to take another."

"Suit yourself," said Maggie, nonchalantly.

We'd been playing the talk about having sex game for about four years now, ever since we almost did so during one rum soaked evening. I'd grabbed her suddenly and we'd kissed passionately for a few moments, but when we'd finally unlocked our lips, we came to the mutual conclusion that it had felt totally weird. So every once in a while now one of us would suggest coupling, as a sort of affirmation of our commitment to not do just that.

Not that Mags (something I never called her to her face, unless I felt like getting punched or pinched incredibly hard) wasn't good looking. As a matter of fact she was, in a clean, athletic, tomboy sort of way. That is, clean when she wasn't covered in grease from tinkering with a boat motor, which just made her attractive in a totally different way. But you either totally clicked with someone or you didn't, and while the two of us got along famously, it appeared we would never get along infamously, no matter how appealing it sometimes seemed to my libido. Which didn't mean she wasn't my girl, however.

"Well, shit," I said. "Maybe I'll do some housecleaning on my boat."

"Something I'm sure it could use," said Maggie.

"Or maybe I'll just take a nap," I said, eying a nearby hammock.

"Yeah, heaven forbid; you actually thought about doing something useful there for a moment," said Mags.

"Close call," I said. I stroked the ever present stubble on my chin in not so deep thought. I never had much of anything to do these days, but today it really felt like I had nothing to do. And it was causing me to get seriously close to doing something.

Just in the nick of time, Maggie put her paper down and came to my rescue. "If you're really that bored, then how about giving me a ride back to Hockeytown?"

"Is your truck broken again?" I asked. "Not very good PR for the island mechanic."

"It's not broken; not right now, anyway, although I'm sure it's only a matter of time since it likes to keep me busy. I just felt like walking over here this morning, but I don't feel like walking back again," said Maggie, standing up.

"Let's go, then," I said, grabbing my white Panamanian hat off the table and sticking it snugly on my noggin. As we walked around the Wreck I peeked in to verify Keyon wasn't napping already, then we got on my Xingfu motorcycle and I started it up.

"I think you just wanted to get your arms around me," I said to Mags over the loud grousings of the old cycle at having to move again.

"Which seemed a little easier the last time we were on this thing," she said, as we slowly pulled out onto the dirt road that wound its way through and around Paradiso Shores. "I could have sworn my hands met without having to give you a python squeeze."

"It's my Hemingweight," I said with a shrug. "For some reason I just keep bulking up; might have

23

the slightest bit to do with my lifestyle. I just figure I'm morphing into Papa H."

We putted along the bumpy path through the palm trees, past little wood homes and the occasional shop. I kept a vigilant eye out for any sudden chicken, pig, iguana, goat, or snake crossings, to avoid any repeat of my past mishaps. There was a not so old saying on Paradiso Shores that Kian had penned; not so old, but true. *"Why did di pig cross di road? To make Captain Harry crash into di tree."* And it pretty much applied to any and all domestic or wild life on the island.

Paradiso Shores had been discovered by another of those lost Italian explorers, Alessio Berardi. Except Alessio stumbled upon his find four hundred years later than the rest of them, in eighteen ninety-two, as opposed to fourteen ninety-two. By then, it was pretty likely others had already been to Paradiso Shores and had perhaps decided it wasn't worth mentioning to the other explorers for fear of being laughed at. And since no one had taken any official credit for it yet, Alessio decided to, and named it on the spot.

The spot his boat had washed up on shore, that is, where he'd ended up after passing out while trying to sail from the Dominican Republic to Puerto Rico after drinking too much sangria. Not quite how Cristoforo did it, but considering all Columbus was looking for was a shortcut when he found the Bahamas and the Virgin Islands, Alessio's discovery method with his own Caribbean paradise was alright.

I had no idea whether or not the whole story was true. But Alessio did at the very least still have a descendent living on Paradiso Shores, Cosimo Berardi. Cosimo strutted around the island like a peacock in an outlandishly bright, sweat stained, old fashioned, yellow suit, while claiming to be in charge of the local mafia and the entire island. He was welcome to govern both as far as I was concerned, as long as he stayed out of my business. Our population was smaller than most Italian families, and his mob consisted of a skinny kid and an ill-tempered Toucan, so his power was tenuous at best. Although I had to admit, that Toucan scared the hell out of me.

Maggie and I quickly arrived at Hockeytown and I shut off my cycle's motor, relieved to have some quiet again.

"When are you going to let me try and jerry-rig a new muffler for this thing?" said Mags, as she swung off the back of the bike.

"When I'm sure I won't need to ride it for a few days," I said.

"You never need it," said Maggie. "The island's not that big."

"Says the girl who just begged me for a ride back here," I said. "Besides, I like the noise; I figure it helps keep mammals and lizards out of my path."

"Suit yourself," said Maggie.

My Xingfu cycle had been on Paradiso Shores sitting covered in Maggie's workshop when I'd arrived, being one of five bi-wheeled vehicles on the island. How a Chinese bike got all the way to the Caribbean was beyond me, but I figured it was fate that we'd met. It may have been one of the most unpopular brand of motorcycles ever built, but I found out the name Xingfu meant *"happiness or contentedness felt through having everything you want in life and not having any looming worries."* That pretty much summed it up for me.

"Since you're so terribly busy today, do you want to help me open the store?" said Maggie.

"You need me to flip the closed sign over again?" I said.

"No, but the awning is still giving me grief," said Mags. "There's a Bloody Maggie in it for you if you help."

I considered tossing out another mechanic joke, but figured I was already too near to going over my daily quota without getting hit, which was one. Besides which, I wanted the Bloody. "Lead the way, m'lady," I said, instead.

We headed towards the center building of Hockeytown, Detroit bred Maggie's nickname for the small complex of brightly painted structures that filled the sprawling fenced in yard on the beach that was both her home and workplace. The small market in the middle was the hub of activity, and a place that most of the people on the island frequented at least once a week for food and other supplies. If Mags wasn't there, you could usually find her either tinkering with something mechanical in the garage on the left side, or in her workshop on the right blowing glass bubbles in the tropical heat.

I had no idea how she did either of her side activities in the temps at this latitude, although she tended to do her glass blowing at night when it was *"cooler"*. She said she just used all the spare comfort degrees she'd banked while living in the north; if seventy-two was optimal for a human, all those below zero days had given her seventy plus degrees each to save for use when it got too hot. Which made sense; back in my old home negative five had surely been the reason I hadn't bitched when the same GPS spot hit the nineties seven months later. But the idea of standing next to that glass furnace for hours still made me about as squeamish as a Popsicle clinging to its stick in fear of falling onto the hot sidewalk.

I walked around the back of the market onto the wood patio, and grabbed hold of the crank that extended Maggie's red and yellow striped awning out over the area. Trying to give it a turn, I found she was right; I had to use the full extent of my beer bottle lifting muscles to get it to move, but it finally grudgingly cooperated. I didn't know why she needed me, though; Mags could twist a bottle cap off a stubborn Landshark with a flick of her wrist, due to all her wrench turning. I suppose she wanted me to feel useful, which was highly unnecessary since I aspired to be anything but. The thought was still appreciated, though, as long as she didn't get carried away.

A few moments later we were sitting out under said awning, a couple of Maggie's secret recipe Bloodys in front of us. Even I didn't know what she put in them; she always whipped them up out of sight in the back storeroom from a large shelf of ingredients, most of which were there just for show so no one knew which ones she actually used. The result was damned good, though, as tasty and complex as a bottle of great Cabernet.

I took a sip, and leaned back and listened to Bob Marley play through the store speakers over the sounds of Mother Ocean as she lazily lapped onto shore beside us. "Why is it when I'm here on your patio it's the best place on Earth, but when I'm home at the Wreck, it is?" I asked.

"Because it's where you are," said Maggie. "No place is perfect unless you're there."

"I'm going to tell everyone you said that," I said.

Maggie thought for a moment. "That's not what I meant," she said, finally.

"Yes it is," I said. "You meant that a place can't be perfect unless *I'm* there."

"For you, not for everyone else!" said Maggie. "You tend to lower the bar for the rest of us."

"Too late," I said. "No take backs. Besides, sometimes the bar needs lowering. It's a lot less work to step over it than to limbo under it."

"Well, you're the right owner for the Rumwreck, then," said Maggie. "If that bar was any lower it would be buried in the sand."

"Thanks; I take that as a compliment," I said, lifting my glass in a toast to myself and the Wreck.

"What don't you?" said Maggie. "By the way, did you hear that Cosimo is looking for contributions for another tourist campaign for the island?"

"Again?" I said. "When's he gonna get it through that fat head of his that we don't want any tourists."

"He does," said Maggie.

"Even if he managed to raise more money than usual, he wouldn't know what to do with it," I said. "He took the few dollars we gave to shut him up him last time and had buttons made up for us to wear that said *"Come to Exotic Paradiso Shores"*. I tried telling him it wasn't gonna help since someone would have to come here first to see them, but he wouldn't listen to me. How much cash does he want this time, and for what?"

"Four thousand, three hundred and seventy-two dollars. And forty-two cents," said Maggie. "For a welcome sign to put on the docks, among other things."

"Which ones? We don't have a public entrance to the island," I said.

"Your docks, I know for sure, since most of the people that come here use them," said Maggie.

"That'll be the day, killer toucan or no killer toucan!" I said. "The last thing I want is for people to get the idea I'm actually glad to have them come and traipse around on my beach. If they insist on going up to the bar that's their business, but I don't want them thinking I'm necessarily gonna like it."

"And that's what makes you such a great and friendly proprietor," said Maggie.

"Damned straight," I said. And another thing-"

I stopped in mid sentence when I heard the sound of an airplane engine off in the distance, growing louder as it approached. It didn't take long for me to figure out who it was by the pitch of the motor, and I stood up, downed the last of my Bloody Maggie, stuck my hat back on my head, and pulled the brim low above my eyes. "I'll see you later, Maggie," I said grimly.

"No way; I'm coming with you," said Mags.

"But you just got here!" I said. "And you just unlocked the store."

"Like anyone's going to show up before Adeline gets here at ten," said Maggie. "And even if someone does and takes something, they'll just leave me an IOU for it."

"Still, it's not really necessary for you to babysit me, you know," I said, as we headed back towards my Xingfu.

"When you're with him, it is," said Maggie.

And I had to admit, she was probably right.

Chapter Three

"Behave," Mags was saying to me, as I headed towards the docks back at the Wreck.

"I might...if he will," I said.

I watched the yellow Noorduyn Norseman aircraft circle and land in the blue-green ocean, then taxi towards one of our docks. I walked over and waited on shore, arms crossed, as the pilot shut down and tied up the plane, then walked down the pier towards me.

"Grizwood!" I growled at him, when he finally came to the spot where the wood meets the sand.

"Captain Harry," said Gus, in an equally unfriendly tone, tugging at his denim cap and stopping just before stepping on shore.

"I see you're still flying that antique," I said, pointing at Gus' plane. "I've got no idea why the laws of physics haven't noticed you up there yet in that Canuckian rust bucket."

"Probably the same reason they haven't made that paper plane of yours drop into the ocean and sink to the bottom where it belongs," said Gus, indicating my own craft, a blue and white American Champion Scout.

"At least my plane wasn't first flown by the Wright Brothers," I said. "Which one was it again? Elmer?"

"Better that than owning an oversized snap tite model that was put together in a basement by some twelve year old cheesehead," said Gus. "Have you replaced the rubber band lately?"

"A lot more recently than you've greased your hamster's wheel," I said.

I loved my new Scout seaplane (it was new when I bought it six years ago, anyway, just before I came to Paradiso Shores), and thought it was a pretty little thing. But if you got right down to the truth of it, I was deeply jealous of Gus' Norseman. The Noorduyn had so much old school thirties and forties style that I would have gladly traded planes with him in a heartbeat. Of course, there was no way I was ever gonna tell the s.o.b. that and give him the satisfaction. Not that he probably didn't already know it, anyway; guys just know when someone is coveting their stuff. But even if he would have been willing to trade, I don't think I could have gone through with it. It would have been like swapping wives; it might sound like fun, but morally, it's just plain wrong.

Gus Grizwood was a commercial seaplane pilot, based out of Tortola on Jost Van Dyke in the British Virgin Islands. And more precisely, the fourth bar stool from the right at the Soggy Dollar Bar. He made a living moving packages and tourists all around the area. You could say the two of us didn't get along, but only if you had a gift for understatement. If I took the time to apply my amateur psychology to it, I'd probably decide it was because we were too damned much alike. And nobody likes a copycat, especially when it feels like they're copying you.

"Now that we've got the aeronautical insults out of the way, we can move on to all the rest. But first, you wanna tell me what the hell you're doing on my island?" I said.

"Can I at least come on shore, first?" said Gus.

"That depends on what the hell you're doing on my island," I said.

"Same son of di beach as always," grumbled Gus.

"Yeah, I am," I said. "Especially when it comes to you. And I thought we decided you were gonna steer clear of here and me."

"We did," agreed Gus.

"I've kept up my end of the bargain," I said. "You haven't seen me near the Soggy Dollar since, have you?"

"No, and I could tell with my eyes closed, since everyone there's been in a really good mood lately," said Gus.

"Judging by your landing, I guess that's how you fly your plane, too," I said. "But you're wasting my time; I've got nothing to do, and I'd rather get on with doing it than jabber with you, so get to the bloody point."

"Fine," said Gus. "Crazy Chester is missing."

"Missing what?" I said.

"Himself," said Gus. "He disappeared four days ago, and no one has seen him since."

"What do you mean, disappeared?" I said. "Disappeared as in poof, vanished?"

"Pretty much," said Gus. "Akiko woke up one morning, and he wasn't there."

"Nothing odd about that," I said. "Chester usually gets up when most people in the islands are just going to bed."

"Yeah, I know, but he wasn't at their bar, or anywhere else on di island, either," said Gus.

"That's odd," I said, thoughtfully.

"So is that a good enough reason to come ashore?" said Gus.

"No, but thanks for playing," I said, pondering the situation. "What about his boat, the Lazy Lizard?"

"Still there," said Gus, from his neutral territory on the dock. "And he didn't leave with Jolly Roger on the shuttle to Tortola, either."

"And you're sure he didn't fly out with you at some point?" I said.

"I think I'd know if Crazy Chester had been one of my passengers, wouldn't I?" said Gus.

"You tell me; as lit up as you get at the Soggy Dollar, you probably wouldn't notice the pope sitting next to you in the cockpit in full regalia," I said.

"Never when I fly!" growled Gus.

"Yeah, I know, so you keep saying," I said, patting myself on the back nevertheless for that one. "So is anyone out looking for him?"

"Roger's keeping an eye out on his run, and I am, too, wherever I end up flying, but that's about it," said Gus. "That's why I'm here, to try and talk you into helping."

"Me?" I said.

"Yeah, you," said Gus. "You think I'd go anywhere near your royal ugliness if I didn't have to?"

"Why me?" I asked.

"Because you have a plane, stupid," said Gus. "I've been looking, but I've got passengers lined up until tomorrow afternoon, now; I just stopped by here on a run to pick someone up in San Juan."

"Poor saps," I said. "You really should have a warning sticker tattooed on your forehead; *"Just because I dress in denim from head to toe doesn't mean I can fly a plane."*

"And you owe him," said Gus, ignoring my latest insult.

"You had to point that out, didn't you?" I said.

"Damned straight," said Gus.

But there was no denying he was right. Not that I probably wouldn't have helped, anyway; Chester was too nice a guy not to drop everything to go in aid of, if he needed it. And considering I didn't have anything to drop, and that he'd saved my life not once, but twice, it pretty much made me the perfect man for the job.

"Alright; I'll do it," I grumbled.

"When?" said Gus. "I promised to let Akiko know; she's beside herself, right now."

"That must hurt," I said. "But I'll leave as soon as I can pack some things and get the plane ready; I'll fly to di island first, and start there."

"Good; then I can get the hell out of here," said Gus.

"Funny, that's exactly what I was going to tell you to do," I said.

Gus waved a dismissing hand at me and headed towards the Norseman, and I headed towards the Anchored Away.

"So I'm sure you heard all that," I said to Mags as I walked up to her.

"I heard," said Maggie. "Believe me, I was listening intently, to make sure you two weren't going to go at it."

"I was on my best behavior," I said.

"That was your best behavior?" said Maggie.

"Yeah, couldn't you tell?" I said with a grin. "Anyway, I think Gus learned his lesson about going at it the last time we did."

"I seriously doubt that," said Maggie. "Boys will be boys, and you and Gus are about as mature as a couple of two-year-olds."

"Ya gotta stay young if you wanna stay young," I said. "Do you want another ride home before I leave?"

"No, I'll walk this time; one round trip a day on that roaring Chinese dragon of yours is enough for my ears," said Maggie.

"Then I guess I'll see you when I get back, whenever that'll be," I said.

"I hope you find him," said Maggie.

"Me too," I said. I went down the dock and stepped onto my floating casa, and eventually remembered where my duffel's place was in my filing system and threw a few of my belongings into it. I didn't plan on being gone for very long; at the very least, I'd come back here and touch base in a day or two to see how things were going. And whatever craziness had led Crazy Chester off to wherever it was he'd disappeared to, I didn't think it would take long to sort it out and find him.

I figured the real reason Gus had come to me for help was that the fisherman had badgered him into it. Obviously having a plane to look for somebody was a plus, but I didn't think for a moment that Grizwood would come near me unless someone forced him to, and the fisherman was fully capable of being pig headed enough to be just that person.

And the fisherman would have done it because besides having the opinion that I should take care of every little problem within a thousand mile radius, he knew if there was one thing that could hold my attention, aside from a beautiful woman with a bottle of rum, it was a mystery. Something in real life, or just a story I was hearing or reading, it didn't matter; like a lot of people, I loved a good mystery.

So I had myself a mini-one now, and it finally gave me something to do. And it even came with an excuse to fly my plane, which was always a plus. And even plus-ier yet, I'd be heading first to di island no less, one of my favorite places on Earth that wasn't within a hundred foot or so radius of where my suntanned carcass usually resided, here at the Rumwreck.

There was, of course, the little matter of Chester's disappearance. Knowing him, it probably was nothing, and he was just being himself, and living his no shoes and no shirt forever, slightly off kilter philosophy on life. Then again, there was the slight chance that something had happened to him, and something not so good or Chester-like.

But I was going to try not to think about that for the moment; I'd store it down in the lower hold of my mind next to the ballast where it belonged. Right now, I was going off on a little adventure to di island, where I'd no doubt see a friend or two of mine.

Except for one.

Chapter Four

"Look, all I'm saying is, you need to take dis very seriously," said the fisherman, for about the twelfth time. And for about the twelfth time this flight, I considered tossing my cell phone out the window of the plane and into the sea, where it belonged.

I'd contemplated chucking it into the drink, or a drink, on numerous occasions before. And on some of them, I'd actually done it. Obviously not with this particular incarnation of the little hand held devil spawn of Graham Bell, since I was talking on it now and it was still functioning. But I'd sent seven of its previous electronic lives down to meet Davy Jones. And, each time, I'd dutifully ordered a new one the next day. I didn't want to, but I needed to stay at least slightly connected to my old world, in case something happened to my sons. Who I still loved, even if they didn't seem particularly inclined to return the feeling.

It wasn't like the thing rang off its metaphysical hook, anyway. It was mostly harmless, spending most of its days lost somewhere on the property until I happened to come across it again, recharge it, check it for messages, move it someplace new, and lose it all over again. Unfortunately I'd decided to bring it along with me on my search, and doubly unfortunately, the fisherman had been sitting with Jolly Roger when I'd decided to call him and ask him a few questions. And now the fisherman was lecturing me over it on the seriousness of the situation.

"It's just I know you, mon, and you never take tings seriously," said the fisherman, which made it thirteen times, more or less.

I looked down at di island and spotted Crazy Chester's bar, and did as low a pass over the upstairs deck as I dared. I could almost see the white of the fisherman's eye (and the black of his patch) as he looked up, and I could hear the audio of my flyover transmitting back from his cell into mine as I roared over his head.

"What di hell was that called!" said the fisherman, a few seconds later, obviously startled.

"It's called, I'm here now, so I'm hanging up before I crash into a palm tree listening to you pontificate, you old coot," I said. "We can finish this conversation on the ground."

"Fine; and I'll have some tings to say to you, you can bet on dat," grumbled the fisherman.

"Like that'll be a first," I said, tapping the end call button.

I circled around di island a couple of times, both to get myself lined up correctly and because I enjoyed looking at the tropical scenery, then glided down and landed smoothly in Mother Ocean (a lot smoother than

Grizwood ever could, in my mind, at least). Then I putted over to Chester's dock where I found Jolly Roger waiting, and he helped me get tied back to land again.

"How you been, Captain Harry?" said Roger, with a handshake and his ever present wide grin.

"I've been me, so I've been pretty damned good," I said. "And you?"

"No complaints, mon, other than I do seem to keep waking up a little bit older every day," said Roger. Then he patted his belly. "And a wee little bit fatter."

I patted my own belly, too. "Only means you're livin' the good life like me."

"Are you two gonna jabber all day down der, or are you comin' up here before di sun goes down?" yelled the fisherman from the upper deck.

I sighed. "You're not old enough to be as inpatient as he is yet, are you?" I asked, as we started to walk towards the bar.

Jolly Roger shook his head. "I don't know where he gets it; most of di older folks around here are as patient as time."

"Hard to say, I guess, since his history is a mystery," I said, striking fear into the hearts of poets everywhere. "For all we know, he used to be Donald Trump's right hand man."

"Hm; di Donald and di fisherman," mused Roger. "Dat would explain di di."

We walked through the lower level of Crazy Chester's bar, coincidentally called Crazy Chester's. By now it was early afternoon, and the lunch crowd was just winding down as the mid-day sitting and drinking crowd meandered in. Unlike my Rumwreck, Crazy Chester's (and di island in general) did a brisk business. His place had that Sloppy Joe's in Key West feel to it, but instead of a Sloppy Rita as a signature drink, Chester's offered the mighty Chesterita. Chester's was also home to the Rum Powered Goats, an island band that played everything from Marley to Mick. And seeing as how they were the only real band on di island, it made the bar a pretty popular place.

"I'm going to find Akiko and see if she needs any help," said Roger, and he headed off towards the kitchen.

I went up the stairs and into the sunlight of the upper patio, and sat down with the fisherman at a table overlooking the ocean, even though it was something I would never overlook. I prepared myself for a lecture, and was surprised when it didn't come.

"Crazy Chester is gone," the fisherman said simply and somberly, instead.

"I know; that's why I'm here," I said. "Was Akiko down in the kitchen? She should probably join us so I can talk to her."

"She is very busy right now; with Chester being gone, she's alone running di bar," said the fisherman. "But I can tell you everyting she knows."

"I guess that'll have to do," I said. "So what happened, anyway? And start from the beginning."

"Where else would I start? At di end?" said the fisherman. "Akiko got up dat morning, at about six o'clock, as she usually does..."

"...and Chester was already gone, as he usually is by that time," I finished.

The fisherman sat back and crossed his arms, but not before adjusting the patch over his right eye into what I always imagined he felt was his angry eye position. "Would you like me to just sit here while you tell yourself what happened, or can I tell di story?" he said.

"Sorry; go ahead," I said.

"Good," said the fisherman, readjusting his patch again. "So Akiko got up at about six in di morning, and Chester was already gone. Are you wit me so far?"

"Yeah, it's so real I almost feel as if I was there," I said. "Continue."

"Akiko went to di bar to begin baking her tarts and tings, but di bar was still locked up, and Chester wasn't inside. She figured he was off doing someting else, getting supplies or some other ting on di island. But soon di other workers began arriving, and none of dem had seen him, either," said the fisherman. "Dey had to open di bar without him, and he never showed up, dat day or any day since."

"And no one else on di island has seen him, either?" I said.

"No one I've talked to," said the fisherman.

"Who have you talked to?" I asked.

"I'm not telling you," said the fisherman.

"What? Why the hell not?" I said. "I don't want to waste my time talking to people who don't know anything."

"Dat's exactly di reason, right der!" said the fisherman. "You be too damned lazy, Harry. You need to talk to everyone, because you never know what dey might know."

"I would know what they'd know if you told me!" I fumed.

"I'm not sayin' another word," said the fisherman, and he closed his eye, and adjusted his patch into its matching position.

I knew from experience that that was that; once the fisherman shut his eye patch I'd get nothing more out of him, even if I sat there and tried for the next five hours.

"So basically I've got to interrogate the whole damned island," I said.

"Except for Akiko, yes," said the fisherman.

I stood up. "I guess I better get started, then, since as it is, I won't be finished until Chinese New Years," I said. "In the year of the wombat, that is. But I'm talking to the head honchos around here first; maybe one of them knows something, and I can save some time."

"Always trying to cut corners, aren't you?" said the fisherman. "Soooo lazy."

"Damned straight," I said. I turned to leave, then remembered Keyon back on Paradiso Shores. "By the way, you need to get your rear back to the Rumwreck asap. Kian has the day off, and once Keyon is done for the day, there'll be no one to watch the place."

"But I was going to stay here for a while and look for Crazy Chester," complained the fisherman.

"Sure you were; you'd be a big help locating him if he wandered back into his bar," I said. "And who's being lazy now? So git."

"I will after you do," said the fisherman.

I put my hands up and said, "Then I'm gone," and wandered downstairs and out of the bar.

And right back into another one, where I fell under the gaze of a salivating simian.

Chapter Five

Monkey Drool's was my kind of place. Hell, I owned that kind of place. Like the Rumwreck, the Monkey occupied its plot of beach with carefree pride, not caring if it too lowered the limbo bar for what a beach bar could be, on down to what it should be. If it was bothering to make a point at all that was the point. Relax, mon, it was saying; we've got every little ting you need. Sand and the ocean, and a place to sit down and enjoy them with a cold beer. And you can just be yourself, because it doesn't matter who you are, you're good enough for this weathered, beaten-up, worn out, comfortable, old flip-flop of a bar.

The Monkey sat a short distance down the beach from Crazy Chester's, looking like a nautical swap meet had washed up on shore and decided to turn itself into a bar. Buoys, broken oars, nets, ship steering wheels, propellers, you name it, it was probably hanging there somewhere. All under the singular eye of the stuffed monkey with the patch and the sombrero, looking like he'd been taxidermied by a blind man with a pocket knife, a hose, and about a hundred pounds of Play-Doh.

It was a likely place to start looking for Chester, since he and the Monkey's owner, the Innkeeper (no relation to the fisherman), had had a long ongoing feud due to Chester's bar and the business it sucked away from the Monkey. I knew the Innkeeper well enough to know that he might very well be capable of foul play, and he took his bar's health and well being very seriously. A lot more seriously than I did, at least monetarily, that was for sure.

I grabbed a seat at the bar down a ways from a trio of touristy looking gents, and waited for the Innkeeper to appear, which he soon did.

"Captain Harry!" he said exuberantly, with a big smile. "Welcome back to my bar. How is my favorite son of di beach?"

"Dying of thirst," I said. The afternoon tropical heat was beginning to kick in, and something cold was sounding very good.

"Di usual, den?" said the Innkeeper.

"Sure; which one of my usuals do you have today?" I asked, knowing the beer selection changed constantly at the Monkey, due to whatever strange ordering system the Innkeeper had.

"I have di Kalik, if dat be okay," said the Innkeeper.

"That'd be perfect," I said. I watched my beer be pulled out of the chilly confines of the cooler and opened, stuffed with a lime wedge, and then placed invitingly in front of me, like a beautiful woman walking into the room and sitting down next to me. In some ways, the beer was even better than a woman, since I knew I was more likely to get what its appearance promised to give me. I took a long sip and verified that fact when it hit my T-spot, and helped continue man's seven thousand year relationship with our yeasty friend.

"Ah," I said. I sat back and checked out my surroundings, while trying to figure out how best to broach the subject on Crazy Chester's disappearance to the Innkeeper.

If it was anyone besides Chester who was missing, I and a lot of people that knew him would have probably chalked it up to some kind of an accident. That sort of thing did unfortunately happen from time to time; an early morning swim in the ocean, a case of cramps or a shark, and Mother Ocean's bosom would have a new permanent house guest. But Chester was one of those people who had things happen to him, and not of the mundane sort like drowning. Besides which, he'd fallen off his boat so many times and survived it was unfathomable to think he would ever die in the sea. So even if it was nothing sinister that had caused him to vanish, and no matter how brief a time it might take to look into, it was worth it because the answer should turn out to be interesting at the very least.

"So did you have anything to do with Crazy Chester's disappearance?" I said to the Innkeeper, deciding to take the direct approach as usual and simply accuse him and get it over with.

"I knew it! I knew di people would tink I had someting to do wit it," fumed the Innkeeper, waving his arms around.

"Well, maybe everyone wouldn't think it if you didn't threaten Chester and his bar at least once a week," I said. "You're more punctual about it than you are with your happy hours."

"Happy hours?" said the Innkeeper, puzzled.

"Never mind; I forgot how cheap you are," I said. "So are you gonna answer the question?"

"I know the same ting as everyone else; one day he was here, and di next day he was not here," said the Innkeeper. "And I had noting to do wit it."

"Nothing, Francis?" I said, using both his real name and the tone I imagined his mother had used with him.

The Innkeeper continued to quietly sulk for a moment, and all I and the three obviously interested and eavesdropping tourists down the bar could hear were the palm trees rustling overhead in the ocean breeze. Then Francis' shoulders slumped, and he sighed. "Well, I may have sort of suggested dat der would be a fat reward if he suddenly wasn't der one day."

"What!" I said. "To who?"

"To two men from Saint Martin...or was it Sint Marteen? I forget which," said the Innkeeper.

"Why the hell did you do that?" I said.

"You need to ask? You just said I threaten him every week, mon," said the Innkeeper.

"Yeah, but that's all you ever did; I didn't think you'd ever go through with anything," I said.

"I didn't tink I would...or did, either," said the Innkeeper. "I was just talking and complaining to dese two like I always do wit people. But den Chester was gone di next day."

I took another big swig from my Kalik and thought things over; this was already seeming more difficult than I would have thought, and possibly more serious. "Have you seen those guys since? I mean, they haven't come back looking for the reward or anything, have they?"

"I haven't seen dem, no," said the Innkeeper. "But I figured dey were laying low, waiting for di heat to cool down."

"Maybe," I said. "Or maybe they had nothing to do with it, and you were lucky and should learn to keep your trap shut."

"You tink so?" said the Innkeeper. He leaned across the bar towards me, and spoke quietly. "Di truth be known, I don't want anyting to happen to di Chester, now. My business has been plenty good since he opened his place; when he get busy, I get busy."

"That's good to hear at least," I said. "Maybe you should tell him that and let everyone else know, too."

"Naw," said the Innkeeper. "People like di feud; dey expect it, even if it doesn't exist anymore, so I have to keep up di appearances."

"If you say so," I said. I grabbed a pen that was lying on the bar, wrote my cell number on a napkin, and slid it over to Francis. "If those two guys show up again, call me right away and let me know what happens."

"Even if Chester is back by den?" asked the Innkeeper.

"No, not if he's already been found," I said. "I could care less then. Unless you want to clue me in on whether it was Martin or Marteen they were from, because I'll be losing sleep over that one."

"I'll do dat den, Captain Harry," said the Innkeeper.

I decided to hang out at Monkey Drool's for a few hours and see what and who happened by. Along with Chester's, it was the center of activity on this side of di island, and a good portion of di islanders you might call the who's who usually came through. There was no point in running around in the heat trying to find everyone I wanted to talk to when they would just come to me, and there weren't many better places to try and solve a mystery than in a beach bar. Even if I had given the fisherman a hard time about wanting to do just that.

Come to think about it, there weren't many better places to do much of anything than in a beach bar, except for maybe feeling depressed; that was a tough one to do with a frosty something in one hand, a jerk chicken leg in the other, and Mother Ocean dancing before your eyes.

And by nightfall, I sported the usual big smile to prove my point.

Chapter Six

"I tink he's hiding somewhere here on di island trying to get some attention," Faith was saying from one side of me at the bar.

"Come on, Faith; it's Chester we're talking about here," Jack Danielson answered from my other side. "The last thing he wants is attention. At least, from anyone but Akiko."

"Maybe on di surface," said Faith. "But deep down, I tink he loves being in di spotlight. You remember his birthday hat he wears every year, don't you?"

"Yeah, how can I forget; it *is* a spotlight," said Jack, describing Chester's Carmen Miranda meets O Tannenbaum chapeau. "Boats steer clear of our shores when he's got it on."

"It's hard to imagine dat someone who puts a lighthouse on his head wants to be ignored," said Faith.

"That is a good point," said Jack.

Jack Danielson owned di Island Rum Company, as well as the Sugar Daddy Plantation here on di island. Not to mention *Jacks,* a tiny shipwreck bar on the equally tiny, neighboring, Isla De Luis. Like me, he too had run away from a home in America. But unlike my departure, his escape from the ordinary had been a long and winding one, involving not-dead ghost pirate uncles and dilapidated rum factories. In the end, though, the result had been the same; his home too was now in the little latitudes, where he counted his lucky stars in his own particular harbor.

Faith was his trusty assistant at the rum factory, a native to di island, and the person who really ran the place; Jack just signed the checks and tried to stay the hell out of the way. He had me beat in that department, since I'd been tricked into actually running the Wreck by the fisherman while he just kicked back and enjoyed himself. Luckily my job didn't entail much more than opening a few beers for friends, something I'd always been willing to do anyway. So I couldn't complain, at least any more than I did about anything else.

"Where's Kaitlyn, Jack?" I asked. "Is she on di island for good yet?"

"One more month," said Jack. "She's in Hawaii right now, finishing up her work, and then she'll finally come back here. And two weeks after that we get married."

"I hope you know what you're doing," I said, motioning to the Innkeeper for another Pickled Parrot, Toasted Toucan, and Cockeyed Cockatiel for the three of us. It was always a fun way to drive a bartender mad, drinking three different complicated drinks.

"I do know; Kaitlyn's the one," said Jack.

"Mine was the one, too. The only one. Fool me once, shame on me. But I'm not gonna be a fool twice, I can guarantee you that," I said. "So how's your uncle Billy? Still crazy after all these years?"

"He's still Billy, and still sailing right along," said Jack. "He had a wonderful run in with Crazy Chester just before he disappeared, by the way. The two really got into it, this time."

"I thought they were best buddies now," I said.

"They are," said Jack. "But evidently chasing Chester's customers around the beach with a dull cutlass will anger even him."

"Now dat was fun to watch," said Faith, with a little giggle.

"Billy did that?" I said, taking a drink of my own Drooling Monkey bird of paradise of choice, the Pickled Parrot.

"Yes, he did," said Jack. "Well, he didn't chase all of them; just a select few, according to Chester."

"I wonder what set him off?" I said. I was now a bit curious if Billy, aka Captain Black Dog the pirate ghost, was playing any part in Chester's vanishing act. I found it hard to imagine, though. While you might say Billy was a little off kilter since he insisted upon dressing and acting like a pirate twenty-four seven after going off the deep end years ago, I don't think there was anyone, including me, who believed he was truly dangerous in any way. Except for maybe the people he'd evidently been waving his cutlass at earlier in the week.

"I tried to talk to him about it, but he just clammed up," said Jack. "And he's been even clammier since Chester disappeared, not to mention downright sulky."

"I'd love to try to get him to tell me about it," I said.

"Go right ahead, although I don't know if it will do you any good," said Jack. "He was lurking around down by the water a few minutes ago if you wanted to talk to him now."

I turned my stool towards the ocean, squinted my eyes, and looked. "I see someone down there, sitting on a log or something," I said. "But I don't know how you can tell if it's him or not."

"You have to wait for the moonlight to hit the waves behind him just right, then you can see the silhouette of his tri-cornered hat," said Jack.

I waited and watched for a few seconds, then said, "Got it; I see the hat now." I picked up my coconut mug off the bar. "I'll be back in a bit, then."

"Good luck; you'll need it," said Jack.

I made my way down towards Billy, half expecting him to bolt and run off like he occasionally did with some people. Usually he seemed reasonably glad to see me, but I had no idea what his mood might be tonight.

"Ahoy, Captain Harry," he said to me somberly, as I grew near him.

"Ahoy, Captain Black Dog," I answered. "How did you know it was me?"

"I could make out the silhouette of your Panama hat," said Billy.

"Ah," I said. "Well, I guess neither of us is going to stay incognito for very long with our headgear."

"Tis true," said Billy. "But a pirate without a good hat is just a swabby."

"And an ex-patriated American without a Panama hat is just an ex-patriated American without a Panama hat," I said.

"Aye," said Billy. "So; you've come to talk to me about Captain Crazy, haven't ye?"

"Now how did you know that?" I said, sitting down next to him on the log.

"That's why ye be here on di island, isn't it?" said Billy, stroking his gray beard. "To look for Chester?"

"Well, I'm not going to ask how you know that, too, but yes, that is why I'm here," I said.

"Dark doings have been afoot," growled Billy. "Fowl deeds took place, in spite of me best efforts."

"What exactly happened, anyway?" I asked, as the ocean ran up and tickled my bare toes where they wiggled in the sand.

"As ya know, I'll forever be keepin' an eye on Akiko," said Billy. "I may be a crusty old pirate, but she's always treated me kindly, and I think of her as the daughter I never had. I figured Chester could take care of himself; and if he couldn't, that would mean he couldn't take care of Akiko either, and didn't deserve her."

Just then my phone decided to ring, and I took it out and glanced at it, didn't recognize the number, ignored the call, and put it away again. "Go on," I said to Billy.

"The day before Chester disappeared, I was keepin' a weather eye on Akiko as usual, this time while she was at the bar. Why he's got her workin' like some servin' wench instead of pamperin' her like a queen at home, I don't know, but she doesn't seem to mind," said Billy. "Anyway, there were these two shady lookin' characters who seemed to be lookin' the place over from a distance."

My phone rang again, I checked and found the same number was calling, and ignored it a second time. "Damn thing," I said.

"You ought to throw that contraption into the sea and let old Hob have it," suggested Billy.

"It rings many more times and I may do just that," I said. "But please, continue, Captain."

"I'd noticed those same two scallywags talkin' to the Innkeeper earlier in the day," said Billy. "That made me suspicious right there. You can't trust any man with a name like Francis."

My phone rang yet again, and I ignored it without looking, and said, "Wait a minute; you said it was the same two men checking out Chester's that you'd seen talking to the Innkeeper?"

"Aye," said Billy. "I was here down on the beach that very day, and I could see they were speakin' in conspiratory tones up at the Monkey."

"How did you know from that distance they were conspiring?" I said.

Billy looked dumfounded at me, then finally pointed at himself and said, "Pirate, mate!"

"Oh yeah; I don't know what I was thinking," I said.

"Neither do I," said Billy. "Anyways, I could tell they were up to somethin' no good, so when they finally went up and grabbed a table and Akiko came over to serve them, I drew my cutlass and charged in before the scoundrels could kidnap her."

"And how did they react?" I said.

"Like the cowards they were, by runnin'," said Billy. "I chased them, of course, but I'm not so fast on land these days; I'm quicker when I'm out on the sea. Anyhow, then Chester came out and started yellin' at me to knock it off, and like an idiot, he apologized to the men and invited them inside the bar."

"That's all very interesting," I said, and was about to ask Billy what the men looked like, when my phone rang yet again. I swore, not so under my breath, yanked it out of my pocket, tapped the answer button hard, and hollered into it, "Who the hell is this?"

There was silence on the other end of the line for a moment, broken by, "It be me; di Innkeeper. You know, at di Monkey Drool's?"

"Oh, you," I grumbled. "What do you want, anyway, and it better be good."

"You know how you told me to call you right away when di two men came back?" said Francis.

"Yes, I still remember, even after all this time," I said, impatiently.

"Well, dey be sittin' at a table up here right dis very minute," said Francis.

"Why the heck didn't you call!" I said, and quickly hung up the phone. "I gotta run," I told Billy, standing up.

"Something amiss?" asked Billy.

"Yeah, I think those same two guys we were just talking about are up at Monkey Drool's right now," I said. "Come to think about it, maybe you should come with me and identify them."

"I don't need to; it's them. I saw them sit down right about the time you got down here," said Billy.

"And you were going to tell me...when?" I asked.

Billy shrugged. "I hadn't gotten to that part of me story yet; sort of came at the end, now didn't it?" he said. "But I was gettin' around to it."

That sort of almost made sense, and I knew enough not to try and argue with Billy anyway. So I snapped off a quick salute goodbye and headed back towards the bar, wondering what I was going to do when I got there.

Chapter Seven

"So who are we talking about here?" I asked the Innkeeper, as I checked out the crowd.

"Dose two; di ones under di nineteen sixty-three Idaho license plate," said Francis.

I looked, and spotted two men in ridiculously loud flowered shirts talking to one another, coconut mugs in hand.

"Those two?" I said. "They don't look like they're from Saint anywhere to me; more like Spokane or someplace."

"Or Mini-soda," suggested Jack, who was an ex Sodian himself.

"Dat's what dey told me, mon," said the Innkeeper.

I watched the two men for a moment, and said, "I suppose I should go talk to them, but I wish I had some backup on the tiny off chance they actually are up to no good. You know, someone who would really intimidate them."

"I'll go with you," said Jack.

I looked him up and down. "What are you gonna do, threaten to tell them your Jimmy Buffett philosophy on life?"

"Dat always scares di hell out of me," said the Innkeeper.

"Very funny," said Jack. "Keep it up, and I may do just that."

"You be pretty intimidating, Captain Harry; you just need to be di son of di beach," said Faith.

"Thanks, but I meant someone who could really scare them," I said. "Enough so I don't have to worry about getting shot again."

"I could run next door quick and get Jedidiah; I saw him go in a few minutes ago," said Jack.

"Perfect," I said. Jedidiah was one of the biggest people I'd ever seen, looking like he was able and liable to pick someone up by their head with the palm of his hand. "But you better hurry up; I get the feeling they're going soon."

"Yah, I tink dey were only gonna have di one," said the Innkeeper.

Jack scurried off towards Chester's while I kept my eye on the two suspects. But just as I'd thought, the men soon finished their drinks and got up to leave.

"Damn," I said, watching them as they walked down towards the water in the opposite direction of Chester's bar. "I guess I'm gonna have to go solo; tell Jack and Jedidiah which way I went."

"You bet, Captain Harry," said Faith.

I hurried down the beach after the men, wondering what I was going to do when I caught up to them. I'd pretty much figured out all the things I wasn't going to do by the time I got to within ten yards of the pair, when I heard a loud shout of, "Avast!" and saw a shadowy figure jump out from behind a palm tree and into their path.

"It's him again!" I heard one of the men say, as they both took a step backwards and towards me. One of them turned as if to run, but spotted my rum enhanced figure coming his way.

"Hold it right there!" I said. "We need to talk."

"About what?" asked the man, worriedly. "Are you with this pirate lunatic?"

"Watch who you're callin' lunatic, lad!" growled Billy. "Or you'll be tastin' cold steel."

"Is it okay if I handle this, Captain Black Dog?" I said.

"That's what I had in mind; I'll just be holdin' them here in case they try and escape like the yellow bellies they are," said Billy.

"Thanks," I said.

"What's this all about?" asked the other man.

"I'll get right to the point," I said. "A friend of ours went missing about a few days ago, and I happen to know the Innkeeper offered the two of you a reward if he disappeared."

"What! What are you talking about?" said the first man.

"You know what I'm talking about," I said. "Maybe you took him to Saint Martin?"

"Or Marteen," said Billy.

"Whatever," I said. "Just tell me where he is, and if he's safe, we won't have a problem."

"You're nuts," said the second man.

"Wait a minute," said the first man. "When you say, the Innkeeper, are you talking about the guy at Monkey Drool's?"

"Yeah, that's him," I said.

"Damn," said the first man. "Scott, don't you remember? The bartender? He was complaining about the guy who owned the bar next door."

"Not really; I was pretty much out of it after all those Chesteritas," said Scott.

"That's what this is all about? And that's why this guy keeps chasing us with a sword?" said the first man.

"Yes; well, this time, anyway. The first time was...never mind," I said.

"Look; I'm sorry if your friend is missing, but Dave and I didn't have anything to do with it," said Scott.

"No, we didn't," said Scott. "You should probably talk to that bartender."

"I did, but he didn't have anything to do with it either, except to shoot his mouth off about it to you two," I said. "You are the guys from Saint Martin, right?"

"From Saint Martin?" said Dave. "Not really. But we were staying there before we came here to di island; Scott and I are hopping around the Caribbean on our honeymoon."

"Oh," I said, then added, "Ohhhhh." Not that I had a problem with whatever anyone wanted to call a lifestyle, but for some reason Dave's statement convinced me they were telling the truth; it just wasn't the sort of thing you made up.

"The Innkeeper probably couldn't understand exactly what Dave was saying, as smashed as he was," said Scott. "Those Chesteritas pack quite a wallop."

"Don't I know it," I said, which I did. "Put away your sword, Black Dog; we've got the wrong men."

"Then who are the right men?" said Billy. "Damn it, I feel like threatenin' someone!"

"I don't know, but it's not these two," I said. "I'm sorry, guys."

"It's alright; we've got a good story to tell our friends at home, now," said Scott. And he and Dave turned and walked away.

I sighed. "Back to square one, I guess," I said, turning to Billy.

"I still think you should've let me threaten them a bit more, just in case," said Billy.

"Next time," I said.

"Hey, I was just thinking," said Dave, who had come up behind me again. "Your friend you said was missing; he was the guy at Crazy Chester's, right? And he disappeared last Thursday, you say?"

"He *is* Crazy Chester," I said. "And yes, he vanished sometime on Thursday."

"That's what I thought you said," said Dave. "I don't know if it means anything, but I did see him Thursday morning, very early. I remember talking to him at the bar the day before; in fact, he was the one who made us our Chesteritas, and rescued us from this pirate guy, here. It's about the last thing I remember from Wednesday."

"And you saw him the next day?" I asked.

"I told ya ye should have let me threaten' them some more!" said Billy.

"Quiet, Black Dog," I said. "Where was this at?"

"On the beach," said Dave, and he looked around, then pointed a short ways down from where we were standing, towards Robichaux's. "I was passed out right about there, my head under that bush."

I walked over to the spot and the others followed. "Here?" I said.

"Yes. It was just past dawn, judging by the sun. He woke me up, to make sure I was alright, and I sat for a few moments and waited for my head to clear," said Dave. "Which didn't happen, of course."

"And then what?" I said. "Did you see where he went afterwards?"

"Yes. He went to the dock in front of that restaurant, Robichaux's, got on a small sailboat, and headed out there somewhere," said Dave, pointing out to sea. "I don't know where to; I got up and left about then. I hope he didn't drown or anything; he seemed like a nice guy, although he might want to put on a shirt from time to time."

"That goes against everything Chester stands for," I said. "But that does help some; it gives me someplace to start looking besides for two guys from Saint Martin."

"I'm glad," said Dave. "I hope you find him."

"Yeah, good luck," said Scott.

The two of them left, and just as they did, Jack sauntered up.

"Where the hell have you been?" I said.

"Waiting for Jedidiah," said Jack. "He was sitting in with the Rum Powered Goats on steel drums; I finally gave up when they started to play Free Bird."

"You're kidding, right?" I said.

"About Free Bird, yeah, but it was obvious he wasn't going to take a break anytime soon," said Jack.

71

"So what's the story? I'm guessing those guys didn't know anything about Chester, did they?"

"Actually, they did, though not in the way I would have thought," I said.

"But we almost didn't get it out of them, because Harry didn't let me threaten them enough," complained Billy.

"What did you find out, then?" asked Jack.

"He left di island on his own; that much we know, now," I said.

"But to where?" said Jack. "Do we even know where to begin to look?"

"Aye, we do," I said. "Captain Black Dog?"

Billy turned, and pointed his cutlass out to sea. "The mysterious Isla De Luis," he said dramatically.

"Mysterious?" said Jack.

"For once, just shut up and don't ruin it, lad," said Black Dog.

And Jack didn't.

Shut up, that is, but Jack can't help being Jack.

Chapter Eight

"So now what?" said Jack, who was still talking, but after a few hours of respite.

"You could get us some beers, since this is the spot for Jack's, and it's your establishment," I said. "It's getting hot."

"I can do that," said Jack, who went off to the bar to do so.

We were out on Isla De Luis, a tiny piece of dry land off the shores of the main island, not even large enough for one piddly Super Walmart. Jack and I had putted out there in the same sailboat Chester had used to try and find more clues to Chester's V-Day, or Vanishing Day, as I'd begun to call it.

I walked around in circles, kicking the sand around with my flip-flops in case there was something dreadfully important buried in it, but found nothing. Scanning the blue-green horizon told me little either, other than that it was pleasant to look at, which was something I already knew.

Jack soon came back with two cold, limey, Coronas and handed one to me.

"Boyd said he told everyone they could just grab his sailboat from the dock at Robichaux's and use it if they needed to run out here and back," I said. "But this time, the boat was still here and he had to swim

73

out here and get it. So what happened to Chester? And what was he doing coming out here that early, anyway?"

"I can probably answer that last part," said Jack. "I told him if he ever needed anything bar related, a few limes or a bottle of our rum, that he could borrow it as long as he didn't wipe out our little supply."

"So he sailed out here to get...something. And then what?" I said, looking around. "He's obviously not still here; there aren't a lot of places to hide, unless you have a secret underground rum storage cellar that only you, Chester, and Jack Sparrow know about."

"Maybe he lashed two sea turtles to his feet to get back to di island, but they didn't cooperate and took him elsewhere," said Jack.

"Or he could have just tried to swim back to shore," I said. "But neither makes any sense; he wouldn't just leave the boat here, now would he? So if he didn't do either, what did he do, and where did he go while doing it?"

"He might have gone swimming when he got out here, though; you know, just because he was hot or something," said Jack. "And he got attacked by Jaws."

"You've got to get your mind out of the movie theater for a minute," I said. "Anyway, I just don't see it; swimming, drowning, sea turtles, shark bait, none of it. And if I don't see it, it didn't happen."

"Then any idea how we're going to figure out what really took place?" asked Jack.

I looked over at Jack's tiny bar, a little thatched roof structure that resembled the Rumwreck, except it was smaller yet and didn't look like it was about to collapse. "Those bar stools look pretty inviting," I said.

"That's your answer?" said Jack.

"Yeah," I said, heading towards them. "I find that my brain works better when my ass is in contact with something; I think it grounds me to the Earth."

"So that's why I feel so much better sitting down," said Jack. "And here I thought I was just being lazy."

"There's a scientific reason and excuse for everything, even being a chronic slackaholic, if you twist the facts enough," I said.

Jack and I went over and sat down, and I immediately felt more focused, since I didn't have to spend so much energy remaining upright. Of course, if I sat on a bar stool for too long, I usually had to focus twice as hard just to stay on it than normal standing. But by that time, standing itself would have become almost a circus act anyway, so I'd still be better off with the sitting.

"How's life back on Paradiso Shores?" Jack asked.

"A lot like Gilligan's Island; we've got sand, sun, palm trees, a couple of pretty girls, and lots of wackiness. About the only thing we don't have are any rich people," I said. "And we have sweat; did you ever notice how no one sweats on Gilligan's Island? All the guys wear long pants because evidently no one ever thought to cut them off, but no one sweats. Hell, the Skipper should be a walking perspiration factory, not to mention about fifty pounds thinner."

"Maybe the Howells made their fortune in the antiperspirant business," said Jack. "Or the Professor whipped something up out of fish livers and agave leaves."

"Helluva product, either way," I said, taking another sip of beer. "I know just being around Mary Ann would get me oozing."

Jack and I were quiet for a moment, lost in fantasies of being on a tropical isle with a pretty girl. Which wasn't a huge stretch of the imagination, given our setting.

"So, is this helping us find Chester?" asked Jack.

"No, but it beats banging our heads against a coconut tree," I said.

"You two dudes are looking for Chester?" said a voice.

I looked at Jack's bartender, who seemed too engrossed in cutting fruit to ask questions. "Uh, yes?" I said, to no one in particular, since that's who had seemed to have addressed us in the first place.

"You won't find him here," said the voice, which now that I was listening, seemed to be coming from above.

I stood, interrupting my brain circuit with the Earth, and took a step back so I could see up on the roof. "Hola," I said, to the long haired and bearded figure sitting cross-legged upon it. "What are you doing up there, Moon Mon?"

"Communing with Sol," said Moon Man. I couldn't see his eyes, since he was wearing round, purple shades, but I imagined they were closed in meditation. "It's my early morning solar recharge."

"I see," I said, which I did. I hadn't known Moon Man for as long as I had most of di islanders, since he had only arrived a year or so ago. But I knew enough to know he usually had a reason, no matter how far fetched, for most everything he did. He was a product of the late sixties and Key West who had never grown out of it, and who had seemed in fact to have expanded on the whole flower child thing. I thought of him as a flower man, a trained professional who took his lifestyle as seriously as that same lifestyle allowed him to take it. I actually respected him for that, being true to his inner callings, although it didn't mean I didn't also think he was nuttier than a fruitcake.

"Crazy Chester isn't here," said Moon Man.

"That much we already know," I said.

"But what you didn't know is where he went," said Moon Man.

"And we know we don't know that, too," I said, squinting up into the sun. "Is there something you can tell us that might be useful?"

"Chill out, my friend; all in good time. I've got your info," said Moon Man. "But you have to promise me something, first."

I sighed. "You're not going to make me agree to cleanse my karma in some weird ritual of yours involving incense and chickens, are you?" I said.

"No, but you could learn a lot from our fowl friends, if you stopped eating them long enough," said Moon Man.

"I might, if they'd stop dipping themselves in barbecue, jerk, and buffalo sauce," I said. "So what do you want me to promise?"

"To take me with you when you go looking for Chester," said Moon Man.

"Careful, Harry," said Jack.

I agreed; taking Moon Man with me, of all things, I didn't need. "Uh, can't we just do the ritual instead?" I said.

"No way, dude; I've got to repair my karma, and the only way I can do that is by helping you on your quest," said Moon Man.

"I don't know what that means," I said. "My karma's pretty much like Swiss cheese, and I'm still kickin', so I don't understand the pressing need to repair one. And I wasn't aware this had turned into a quest all of a sudden."

"Promise you'll bring me along, and I'll explain everything," said Moon Man.

It didn't look like I had much choice. "Fine; I promise that if what you tell me gives me some idea where to go next, I'll bring you with me," I said. "But no farm animals in my airplane."

"Fair enough, dude," said Moon Man. He stood up and moved to the edge of the roof nearest me and sat down, his bony, long legs dangling off the edge. "See, I was up here that morning when Chester arrived. I was deep in my commune with Sol, so I saw him, yet didn't really see him, you know? Like with my third eye."

"Happens to me all the time, but usually when I drink Mezcal," I said.

"Exactly," said Moon Man. "I saw him tie up Boyd's boat, head towards the bar, and disappear inside. But when he came back out, it was with two men I'd never seen before."

"They'd been inside the building?" said Jack. "What were they doing in there? That's for employees only, and it wouldn't even have been open yet."

"They must not have read your *"Keep Out"* sign you keep insisting will actually keep anyone who happens across the island out," I said. "Wait a minute; these guys you saw weren't two very white dudes with a pinkish farmer hue, wearing bright, flowered shirts, looking like they didn't come from Saint Martin, were they?"

"No, man; these guys looked to me like they *could* have been born on Saint Martin, or anywhere else in the Caribbean," said Moon Man. "All three of them went and got into a speed boat that was tied to a tree on shore, pushed off, and took off in that direction," he said, pointing to the east.

"Chester just ran off with them?" I asked. "Did it seem like he knew them?"

"Chester treats everyone like he knows them, so it was hard to tell," said Moon Man. "But something tells me he didn't, at least before that morning. The same thing that's been telling my karma I should have stopped him from getting in that boat with them. And now he's missing, and it's my fault."

"And all you know is they headed east?" I said, and I looked out to sea in that direction. "It's a damned big ocean. How are we supposed to know where they ended up?"

"Would it help if I noticed one of the men had a staff shirt from the *Half There Bar* on Jost Van Dyke?" asked Moon Man.

"Maybe," I said. "If you did notice that, that is."

"I did, and that the other guy had a hat from the Soggy Dollar." said Moon Man.

"You saw all that with your third eye?" I said. "That's more than I see with my first and second."

"That's because your first set is used to looking instead of seeing," said Moon Man. "With your third eye, you see the big picture, and that includes all the little details your physical eyes don't pay attention to because they're so bored with them by now."

"Pretty handy," I said.

"I can teach you to use it, if you like," said Moon Man.

"No thanks; I'd have a hard time finding a one lensed pair of shades for it once I pried it open," I said, then I looked out at Mother Ocean again. "Well, that helps a little, but damn. Jost Van Dyke may not seem that big, but that's Gus' turf, and while I ain't afraid of him, I don't want to start something by stumbling all through it searching if I don't have to. So unless we know for sure the one guy works at the Half There Bar..."

"He does," said Jack's bartender, suddenly.

Jack and I looked at him. "You know something, Toby?" asked Jack.

"I didn't want to say anyting," said Toby. "I thought I might get into trouble, Jack."

"What is it?" said Jack.

"Di two men are friends of mine; Leo and Tion," said Toby. "Dey boated over to see me from Jost dat day. Dey were only gonna stay for a couple of hours, but dey got to be havin' a good time, and stayed too long."

"Too long?" said Jack.

"Yeah, mon; dey had to work di next day, and kept saying dey'd be leaving any minute now," said Toby. "But dey were still sayin' it when I closed up di bar, so I said dey shouldn't try to boat back home after all di beer and rum, and dey agreed. Den we stayed up even later out here partying after I finished closing, and dey passed out in a couple of hammocks. So I left di door to di bar open in case it rained so they could hide from it in it, and went home to di island. Den I overslept di next morning, and when I came back out here..."

"They were gone," I finished for him.

"Yeah, mon," said Toby. "I'm sorry, Jack; I know you said to never leave di bar open. But we did pay for di beers we drank. And it did rain dat night, so dat's why dey went inside."

"No problem, Toby," said Jack. "If you trust your friends, it's not a big deal."

"I'd have to tink about dat," said Toby. "I've been wondering if dey made it home, though, and was a little worried, but now I tink maybe dey were still tipsy and Chester drove dem back."

"Why would he have done that?" said Moon Man, hanging his head down over the edge.

"You have to ask?" said Jack. "Because he's Chester; he's like the Dudley Do-Right of the Caribbean."

"The who?" said Moon Man, looking puzzled.

"Dudley Do-Right. You know; Nell, Snidley Whiplash, Inspector Fenwick..." said Jack, trailing off. "Nothing?"

"No clue," said Moon Man, shaking his head. "But don't sweat it, dude; must have been during one of *those* years."

"So we can find your one friend at the Half There if he's working?" I asked.

"Tion, yeah," said Toby. "Maybe he can tell you where Crazy Chester went after dat."

"Why don't we just call the bar?" asked Jack.

"Too easy, and I'd rather talk to someone in person," I said. "Besides, Chester's not here in any case, which means he's still out there somewhere," I added, indicating the far horizon.

"True, but I'm going to call anyway when I get back to di island and find my phone," said Jack.

"You're not coming with us?" I asked.

"I would, but I've got a new rum being born today at the factory, and I like to be there for all the births," said Jack. "Makes me feel like I have a purpose in life."

"I'll let you know if and when I find anything out," I said. "But we should get headed in that direction as soon as Moon Mon levitates himself down here."

"My karma's too messed up to levitate right now," said Moon Man, as his footsteps padded across the roof towards the ladder. "I almost broke my ankle the other day trying it."

I had my course plotted to my next destination, along with another reason to get in my plane and leave the Earth. Not that I ever needed one, mind you; meandering aimlessly around doing the Caribbean Amphibian thing never hurt anyone, unless you were one of Gus's passengers.

And if I got lost this time, which did very occasionally happen if I just followed my nose from island to island, I'd have a passenger who was on a first name basis with the sun and the moon and the stars.

Even if he did sometimes have trouble remembering his own name.

Chapter Nine

Banking off of a northeast wind, I sailed on the summer breeze towards Jost Van Dyke. I of course had my copilot beside me, which would have been handier if we were flying the space shuttle, since he was an experienced space cadet.

Flying over a Caribbean ocean is an amazing experience, one that many people never get to truly approach. Except for perhaps during those handful of seconds when their jet finally gets down under the clouds, right before landing on a St. Somewhere. That is, if you're even lucky enough to be crammed into a porthole seat, as opposed to being crammed between two people in the middle, or sitting on the aisle taking elbow and knee abuse from the beverage cart. Looking out of my side window, I was greeted by that usual unusual view of dancing, shimmering shades of blue and green, wearing little white sailor caps. No dolphins, porpoises, or whales were in sight this time, but a few white boats made their way along the ocean's songlines.

"Why would Chester have gone all the way to Jost when he had to open the bar that morning?" said Moon Man. "And how was he planning on getting back?"

"Good question," I said, thinking it over. "He might have been planning on catching Jolly Roger's shuttle out of White Bay on its return trip to di island; he would have had plenty of time to make it, although he still wouldn't have been back in time to open. Then again, knowing Chester, he probably hadn't thought that far ahead."

"Or maybe he was going to look for Gus at the Soggy Dollar," suggested Moon Man. "He would be in the same area as the shuttle."

"I hope he was smarter than that," I grumbled.

"You and Gus don't get along very well, do you?" said Moon Man.

"You noticed that, did you?" I said. "How very perceptive of you; must have seen it with your third eye."

"What's the problem?" said Moon Man.

"He's him, and I'm me," I said. "You didn't see Kirk and Khan ever make up, did you?"

"Who?" said Moon Man.

I looked at him. "Seriously; doesn't that eye get any TV reception?" I said. "Anyway, Gus and I just don't mix, like oil and water; let's just leave it at that."

"But oil and water can coexist peacefully," said Moon Man. "You don't have to become one to get along."

"Bad example, then," I said. "How about fire and gasoline? We're both fine, as long as you don't put us together."

"You two dudes should just mellow out and learn to be friends; like John said, all you need is love," said Moon Man.

"But I'm not a walrus," I said.

"No? Well, Marley said to get together and feel alright," said Moon Man.

"I'm not a Rastafarian either, but you're in the right climate now, at least," I said, checking my altitude and preparing to set down in the ocean.

"Then what are you?" said Moon Man.

"I don't know, but whatever I am, it doesn't include getting along with everybody just because it would be really nice if the world worked that way," I said.

"It would work that way if you did," said Moon Man stubbornly.

"Yeah, that makes a lot of sense; I would love everyone if I did. Anyway, I really wish we could go on and on about this forever and ever, but my plane would run out of gas and we'd crash into the water and die no matter how much positive thinking I did about it not needing fuel," I said. "So I'm going to land now, if that's okay with you, John, and Bob."

"Alright, but you never know until you try," said Moon Man.

"I'd love to have the satisfaction of saying I told you so after we gave it that shot, but I'd be too dead, so I'm not going to argue with you," I said. Instead I got lined up for my approach and was soon passing from the air into the water, doing another of those many things we do every day that we fail to notice how incredible it is that we can do it at all. And moments later we stood on the shores of Jost Van Dyke, having successfully completed our island hop.

"So where is this place we're going to?" I said. "And why is it that you know where it is but I don't?"

"I can't say why you don't know, but I know because I've been there," said Moon Man. "I've spent quite a lot of time of in the British Virgin Isles."

"I've been there, too, but I can't remember where it is because the time I've spent in the British Virgin Islands has been at the bars, like the one we're looking for, and that tends to cloud your memory," I said. "And I'm beginning to wonder just how old you are; you seem to have spent quite a bit of time pretty much everywhere doing pretty much everything. So which one are you; Merlin or Gandalf?"

"Who?" said Moon Man.

I gave him yet another sideways look; if things kept up, I was going to get a stiff neck.

"I'm just kidding," said Moon Man, with a smile. "It is fun to see your reaction, though."

"Yeah, I'm an easy target," I said. "Well, if you're not going to use your wizardly powers, let me try mine. If I was me, and I was standing right here and wanted to go to the bar, it would be..." and I closed my eyes, then opened them, turned, and pointed. "That way," I said.

"Far out, man," said Moon Man. "How'd you do that?"

"It's a gift," I said. "One of my many super powers, most of which involve rum." I took two steps onto the beach, kicked off my flip-flops before they got overloaded with sand and blew out, then picked them up and continued onwards.

I think one of the reasons walking in the sand is so enjoyable, besides the fact that it's usually next to the water (unless you're in the habit of parading around in your cat's toilet), is that your skin is in contact with literally thousands of little objects. I can't think of any other time it happens, and I get the feeling it excites your body to have so many individual tickling sensations shooting over its nerves at once. Walking in the rain is the only thing that even comes close, but most people race right through that instead of taking the time to savor it. I suppose it's because while schmoozing with the rain you tend to end up good and wet, and for some reason that's a cultural no no when you're about to step into a Cub Foods.

We made our way down the beach past the bikini exhibitions on their towel displays. By the time we got to the Half There Bar I could have happily plopped my arse down in the sand a dozen or so times, and not just because of the bikinis; it just seemed like the place to be, lying there baking under Sol. But by now, I knew better. Almost every place in the tropics was the place to be. Which was probably a major reason people didn't move very fast down here. The spot you're at is usually plenty good, and you're just not in that great a need to be somewhere else.

"Let me do the talking," I said, as we walked beneath the wooden archway that led from the part of the beach that wasn't the Half There Bar onto the part of it that was.

"As long as you don't do the yelling, too," said Moon Man.

"Why would I do that?" I said. "As far as we know, Chester came here on his own accord. Let's just see what Tion has to say."

We walked up to the bar past the usual tropical watering hole array of eclectic island art, beer signs, and yet more bikinis, some still inhabited by their owners, but many hanging from the rafters as if taken as prizes by a cabana boy raiding party. The Half There

91

was nothing extraordinary, which meant I could only sit there for hours without feeling the need to move on, as opposed to places like the Soggy Dollar where I could happily spend the rest of my life if Gus and my liver allowed it. "Is Tion working today?" I asked the bartender.

"Yeah, he's over there," he said, pointing at a young man carrying a case of Red Stripe towards a girl near where we'd come in, who was selling beers to the beach people out of a big steel tub filled with ice.

I caught up with him as he began ripping the box open, and said, "Are you Tion?" since humans are simply incapable of taking someone's word for something.

"Yeah," he said, handing the bottles to the girl, two at a time, as she plunged them into the ice. She was young and pretty, in a *"I sell cold beers on the beach in a skimpy t-shirt and shorts"* sort of way, which was always appealing to guys like me. Or more likely, most all guys.

"I'm Harry, and I'm looking for Chester from di island," I said, wishing as usual that my name didn't mean two things, even if I was actually a bit hairy. But it wasn't like I needed to announce it to new people I met. "We think he may have given you and your friend Leo a ride back here a few days ago from Isla De Luis?"

"Ah, yeah, mon! Of course I remember him," said Tion. "Very nice guy. He found Leo and I sleeping it off in di back of Jack's, and he offered to drive us here since we were still feeling out of it dat morning. I couldn't believe how cool dat was. And den he fell off di boat on di way here."

"He drowned?" said Moon Man, shocked.

"I guess you don't know Chester as well as you think you do; he's always falling into the water," I said. "Is that what you meant?"

"Yeah, Leo's hat blew off, and Chester stood up quick and sort of half jumped and half fell off di boat and into di ocean after it," said Tion. "I had to reach up and throttle down or di boat would have left him behind. Den we went back and got him."

"That's Chester, alright," I said. "So what happened to him? We haven't seen him since."

"No way!" said Tion, seemingly genuinely worried. "I don't know; he said he was gonna catch di ferry back to di island. Di same one I should'a caught when I came dere and will next time."

"That's what I figured he was going to do," I said. "See? I told you he knows better than to get in Gus' plane."

"Yeah, yeah," said Moon Man. "But he didn't get on the ferry, either, unless he fell off that, too."

"I doubt it; Jolly Roger likes to sell all the tickets himself, and walk around before departure and make sure everyone is set to go. He likes people, and meeting them, for some reason. So there's no way Chester could have been on board without him knowing it," I said.

"Then where did he go?" said Moon Man. "Do you recall anything else, Tion?"

"Let me tink," said Tion. "Wait a minute; I remember, now. He asked me if dere were any good jewelry stores near di Half There. I told him I didn't know, but dat I knew a man who usually had some good deals."

"Good deals? On what? Did Chester say what he was looking for?" I said.

"No, only dat he wanted to buy some jewelry," said Tion.

"What, is he going to get some gold chains to bling up, since everyone complains about him wearing no shirt while delivering food and drinks?" I said.

"Maybe he's going to get his belly button pierced," said Moon Man.

"Worse yet," I said, shuddering. "And that's the last you saw of him?"

"Yes," said Tion. "I offered to pay for his ferry ride home, but he wouldn't take it. I would have stuffed di money in his shirt pocket, but he didn't have a shirt.

Den he headed off to look for di man I told him about, I tink."

"Where can we find this guy?" I asked.

"He's usually hanging out around di parking lot behind dis one liquor store," said Tion. "I don't know his real name, but he always wants people to call him di Fox."

"He sounds really reputable," I said.

"Naw, he's definitely not dat. But he does have good prices," said Tion. "Just go out to di street, and follow it right, and you'll come to Benny's Island Liquor about six blocks down and up on di hill."

"Thanks," I said, and for the first time in my life, I headed towards a liquor store with no intention of buying liquor.

Chapter Ten

We found Benny's without much trouble, although walking down a sidewalk for the first time in a year or so made my feet wonder what had happened to all the sand and grass they were used to being treated to. And when we arrived, it didn't seem as if we were in the nicest neighborhood on Jost Van Dyke; there wasn't a lot of crime in the British Virgin Islands, but if it was going to take place, it felt like we might have found the best spot for a photo opportunity with a local villain.

There was a beaten up chain link and wood slat fence around the back of the store, and we went through the gate into the back lot. A picnic table sat to one side, probably for employees to take a break on, and upon it sat a small man in white sunglasses and shoes, wearing red pants and a bright yellow silk shirt. The area may have been out of sight and out of mind of the street, but it seemed his attempt at being inconspicuous ended there and not at his wardrobe.

"Hey, dudes," he said, in a sort of American oriental island dialect. "You two dudes looking for something?"

"Someone," I said, trying to figure out if he had room on his tiny person for anything that might go boom and put another hitch in my step. "I think it might be you; are you the one they call," and I had to stop myself from an involuntary guffaw, "the Fox?"

He got up off the picnic table and onto the cement, which I could have sworn actually made him shorter. "Yeah, dude, that be me," he said, running his fingers through his hair with both hands. "It's because I'm foxy, you know, dude? And smart, like a fox."

I wondered briefly if he had a nineteen seventies Saturday Night Live highlights tape back at his chick pad, because it seemed like he was about to break out in a wild and crazy Festrunk brothers act.

"And people think I'm strange," Moon Man said, leaning over and whispering into my ear.

"Quiet," I said. "And you are."

"So what you dudes need? Shades? Some party treats? Jewelry? Music CD's?" he said. "The Fox got the Gangnam Style, nineteen different versions," he added, starting to dance and hop around the lot and hum before I could stop him or ask him to shoot me instead.

"So you do sell jewelry," I said.

"Yeah, the Fox got the best stuff at low, low, best prices," he said. "What you need? Watches? Gold chains? Rings?"

"Actually, I'm just looking for someone," I said.

"Hey!" he said, putting his hands up in dismay. "What the Fox look like? The internet? The Fox ain't in the information business, dude!"

I sighed. "Look, he came to see you a few days ago. A little guy? A bit taller than you, and-"

"You saying the Fox is little, dude?" said the Fox, defensively.

"No, never," I said. "But *he* is. He wouldn't have been wearing a shirt or shoes, and he would've been shopping for jewelry of some kind. And his name was Chester."

The Fox paused and looked at me as if something I'd said had struck a chord, but then he said, "The Fox don't know nothing," he said. "Nothing! And if he did, he wouldn't tell you. Bad business to talk about customers."

"So you do know something," I said. "Just tell me, and we'll get out of your hair."

"You get out of my hair anyway," said the Fox, waving his hand at me. "The Fox is through with you dudes."

"We can't leave until we know what happened to Chester or where he went next," Moon Man said to me.

"I know!" I said irritability, something I was good at. I got my wallet out of my back pocket and looked inside, and said, "Tell you what; I'll give you ten, make that twenty dollars if you'll just tell me what happened when Chester came to see you."

"No way, dude!" said the Fox. "Now you go now!"

"Well, we couldn't go now later, could we?" I said. "It would have to be now. I mean, if we go now, it would be now."

"What?" said the Fox. "You making fun of the Fox?"

"I don't think you should aggravate him any more," said Moon Man. "Try being nice and see what happens."

"Fine, I will," I said, then put my wallet away and turned back to the Fox. "Look, you little twerp, tell me what I want to know or I'm gonna stick you in that dumpster over there."

"That was being nice?" said Moon Man.

"For me in this situation, yes," I said.

"So, you think you big tough guy? Wanna party?" said the Fox, strutting around and gesturing *"come on"* at me with his hands.

"Careful," said Moon Man.

"You got it, dude," I said, ignoring the warning and starting to move towards the Fox. At which time I got a flashback to another fine mess I'd gotten myself into, when the Fox whipped a small silver pistol out of the back of his pants.

"Ah, you not so tough now, are you?" he said, waving the gun at me Pulp Fiction style. "Now the Fox tell *you* what! You dudes turn around and get against that fence. Then the Fox take all your money, and then maybe he get medieval on you and pop a cap in your buttocks. Move!"

"You see what happens when you don't control yourself?" said Moon Man, as we turned and walked over to the chain link fence and leaned forward against it. "Peace and love are the answer."

"Shut up," I said. I grabbed a couple of links with my fingers and tried to figure out what to do next, as I felt the Fox take my wallet out of my back pocket.

"You big guys always think you John Wayne," said the Fox from behind me. "Well, the Fox, he Vincent Vega. He has the Gangnam Style. He lean, mean, fighting machine. He-"

Suddenly became quiet, as I heard the sound of breaking glass.

I turned slowly around, only to find Gus holding the neck of a dripping, broken liquor bottle, standing over the Fox's unconscious body where it lay on the pavement.

"Grizwood!" I growled.

Chapter Eleven

"You want to explain what you're doing on my island?" said Gus. "Besides pissing off petty local gangsters?"

"I didn't know I was supposed to stay off all of Jost," I said, while leaning down and getting my wallet back from the Fox, as well as Moon Man's macramed one and handing it to him. "I thought I was to stay clear of the Soggy Dollar."

"I can't go to Paradiso Shores at all other than to drop off packages on the dock, so why should you be able to set foot on any of my land?" said Gus.

"Oh, because it's about ten times bigger than Paradiso?" I said, possibly exaggerating a little.

"Hey, it's not my problem you live on such a pimple of an island," said Gus. "Move to a bigger one if you don't like it."

"Man, you two are such a drag," said Moon Man. "Captain Harry, we both just escaped death! We're alive! And Gus here saved us."

"I didn't save him," said Gus, pointing at me with his bottle half. "I saved you, Moon Man; I just couldn't take the chance he might not shoot Harry first, or I would have waited."

"What are you doing here, anyway, Gus?" I said.

"Buying liquor; what else would anyone be doing at a liquor store, dumb dumb," said Gus, indicating his bottle, or what was left of it.

"There's got to be a closer place than this to your stomping grounds," I said.

Gus held up his bottle again. "This was a bottle of Ron Abuelo Centuria Reserva; thirty year old rum, wasted rescuing you from your own stupidity," he said, looking at it as if he were about to cry before tossing it against the base of the fence. "They didn't have it in my neck of the woods, but someone said they had a bottle here. One bottle. I was going to use it to celebrate my, um, birthday."

"Is it your birthday?" said Moon Man. "Happy birthday, dude! Must be a big one...like your fiftieth, maybe?"

"You're supposed to be polite and say fortieth," said Gus. "But yeah, next week."

"Cool! Many happy returns, dude!" said Moon Man.

"I hate to break this up, but we've got an unconscious guy lying here on the ground," I said. "I could care less about him at this point, but I don't want to end up in the Jost police station answering a bunch of questions."

"Yeah, the fuzz can be such a drag," said Moon Man.

"Then let's get the hell out of here," said Gus.

"I'd like to, but I'm pretty sure this guy knows where Chester is, and won't tell us," I said. "Or at the very least, he knows something about it. That's what we were doing when he went all gangster on us."

"Hmm; let me think," said Gus. "I got an idea; let me handle this." And he got out his cell phone and dialed a number.

About an hour later, the four of us were flying over the ocean in Gus' plane, despite my reservations against ever doing just that. Gus had called a taxi and we'd poured the Fox into it in the guise of a drunken, passed out friend, then we'd poured him out again and back into the cockpit of the Norseman.

"Is this guy ever going to wake up?" I asked, looking at the Fox where he sat next to me in the back seat.

"I hit him pretty hard," said Gus. "I guess I don't know my own strength."

"I do, and it's not worth writing home about," I said. "Give me your Guava juice, Moon Man."

"But I'm drinking it!" said Moon Man. "It helps keeps me regular."

"You'll never be regular," I said. "Anyway, it's an emergency."

"Fine," he said, passing it back to me. I poured a bit into my hand, then tossed it onto the Fox's face. He jumped immediately, and looked around, obviously not knowing where the hell he was.

"Where the hell am I?" he said, confirming my suspicions.

I handed the rest of Moon Man's juice back to him, and said, "You're on flight six six six, on *You're Gonna Talk Or Else* Airlines. So I suggest you start doing just that."

The Fox reached behind him towards where he kept his gun, but naturally we weren't polite or stupid enough to have put it back there again for him, and had in fact dropped it out the window of the plane and into the ocean. "You dudes are crazy," he said. "Take me back to the ground."

I shook my head. "Nope. First you have to tell us where Chester went, or you're gonna do a quintuple back flip into Mother Ocean."

"I can't tell you that; if the dude's still missing it's not something I wanna get in the middle of," said the Fox. "I could end up dead."

"Which means you do know something," said Gus, from the pilot's seat. "And you might end up dead anyway; that shirt might be ungodly bright, but I don't think it'll work as a shark repellant."

"This is so wrong," said Moon Man. "My karma's gonna be sooo messed up."

"Life gets messy sometimes; remember, it's for Chester, so just stay the course," I said. "Last chance, the Fox; you gonna talk, or not?"

The Fox looked at me and around the plane, trying to sum up the situation. "Naw; no way, dudes," he said finally, crossing his arms defiantly. "You not gonna open the door up here and throw me out of the plane."

"No?" I said. "I guess you're right."

"I knew it!" said the Fox. "You all talk."

"I wouldn't go that far," I said. "Gus? You wanna take us to the feeding grounds? You know the spot."

"You got it," said Gus. He turned the wheel, and began banking us slowly downwards.

The Fox looked out of the window, and said, somewhat nervously, I thought, "Where are we going, now?"

"Just a little place we know of; somewhere we go to get rid of things we don't need and help the environment at the same time," I said.

"We're gonna help the environment?" said Moon Man. "Far out. That'll help my karma a bit."

Gus soon landed us in the ocean, more smoothly than I would have expected, then drove slowly across the water for a bit before shutting off the engine. He turned around in his seat, and said in his best eerie voice, "We're here!"

"Where are is that?" asked the Fox.

"Out in the middle of nowhere; a place the sharks like to gather and feed," I said.

The Fox peeked out the window again. The water in the flats where we were floating couldn't have been more than ten or so feet deep, crystal blue, green, and clear. It was a truly beautiful place, but whether the Fox would think so or not was unclear at first. "Those are sharks?" he said at last. "They aren't so big."

"Neither are you; it's a match made in heaven," I said, getting up and unlocking and opening the back hatch. "Time for you to get out," I added, indicting the open doorway.

"I thought we were helping the environment," said Moon Man.

"We are; the Thresher Shark population is dwindling, and we're gonna give them a bite. Or I guess, they're gonna give him one," said Gus.

"You won't do it," said the Fox.

"Wanna bet? I'll be doing the world a favor and saving the next tourist," I said. "Can you swim?"

"Yes," said the Fox.

"Too bad. It would be quicker if you drowned; it might take them a while to eat you. But once word gets out there's a meal it should speed things up," I said.

"Why you wanna know about this guy so bad?" said the Fox.

"Because he's a friend; maybe if you had any you'd understand it better," I said. "And he saved my life twice, so trading you for him is no big deal for me. So what's it going to be? You want to spill your guts now, or should we have the sharks do it for you?"

"Fine! I give up," said the Fox, putting his hands up in exasperated surrender. "Though I still don't think you would have thrown me out."

"Well, we'll never know now, will we?" I said. "So what happened with Chester?"

"He came to me and wanted a ring," said the Fox.

"What kind of a ring?" asked Gus.

"I don't know; a nice ring for his girlfriend," said the Fox.

"For Akiko? Then I bet he was looking for an engagement ring. And he came to you? What the hell was he thinking?" said Gus.

"He trusts people. And as far as thinking, he usually doesn't. If Tion told him this guy was someone good to see for a ring, Chester would toddle right off to him without considering the consequences," I said.

"I showed the dude what I had, but most of it wasn't good enough for him," said the Fox. "But there was one special ring I had that he liked, but I told him the diamond was flawed."

"You told him that?" I said.

"Hey, the Fox honest business man!" said the Fox.

No one said anything, and we all sat staring accusatorily at the Fox.

"Okay! He spotted it," said the Fox. "It was a pretty big flaw. I got it cheap and thought I could pass it off to someone, but they always see it."

"So then what?" said Gus.

"He say maybe he buy it, and maybe get another stone for it. He said his girl has green eyes, so he wanted to get an emerald," said the Fox.

"Akiko does have really green eyes," said Moon Man.

"Yes, she does," I said. "Very pretty ones."

"Like a bottle of Heineken," said Gus. The three of us, including the Fox, looked at him. "Well, they are!"

"Very poetic," I said.

"Can I finish? I want to get away from you weirdos," said the Fox.

"By all means," I said.

"I wanted to make the sale, so I tell him where he can get a stone, too, and cheap," said the Fox. "So he goes to the bank and gets the money and comes back and buys the ring, and then leaves."

"And that was it?" I said. "Where did he go next?"

"That's the part I didn't want to tell you," said the Fox. "He went to see the guy I told him about; the guy with the stones. And he a baaaaad man."

"So Chester was working his way up the criminal ladder," I said. "That's just great. And I bet you didn't tell Chester how baaaaad this guy was, did you?"

"No way, dude; I don't mess with this guy. He even more dangerous than the Fox. I just get stuff from him from time to time," said the Fox.

"I don't suppose we have any choice but to go look for him," I said. "So where can we find *this* guy? And what's his name?"

"His name is Luis," said the Fox. "And you can find him in Cuba; I think."

"Cuba? What the hell?" said Gus.

"I hear later that Luis has left the Virgin Islands and taken your friend with him," said the Fox. "Back to his home in Cuba."

"Why would he take Chester with him?" I said. "If something went wrong, then why wouldn't he just shoot him or something and be done with it like a normal bad guy?"

The Fox shrugged. "I don't know; that's just what I hear. Maybe he's holding him for ransom?"

"Or maybe he want's Chester's secret Chesterita recipe," said Gus. "But he'll die before he'll talk."

"I'm not sure what the hell to do now," I said. "What part of Cuba would we find this guy in?"

"He has a big hacienda outside of Matanzas, about fifty miles to the east of Havana along the coast," said the Fox.

"Wonderful; you've been a big help," I said.

"Then can I have the twenty dollars you promised me back at Benny's lot for the info, now?" said the Fox.

"Yeah, right," I said. "That's almost funny enough to make me give it to you. Gus, let's take this idiot back and drop him somewhere."

"Sounds good; I'm thinking on the far side of the island from Benny's," said Gus.

"Great idea," I said.

"You guys never gonna do business with the Fox again," said the Fox, sourly.

"What a shame," I said. "And I was going to come and see you if I ever lose my mind and decide to get married again."

"Really?" said the Fox hopefully.

"Nope," I said. And I closed the hatch as Gus started the engine.

The Tarpon that were feeding in the flats were probably disappointed that they didn't get a little Fox to nibble on. Maybe there had been a few sharks in the area trolling around, but Gus or I knew would know; only that Gus liked to fish there. Not that a gangster in the back lot of Benny's could tell the difference between one fish and another, of course.

I didn't have a clue what we'd do next about Chester's migration to Cuba, but I was surprised by the action that we ended up taking. Not so much by the fact that we went to a bar to think things over, but that Gus suggested the Soggy Dollar, his personal fortress of non-solitude.

But I guess wartime can make allies out of even the coldest of tropical warriors.

Chapter Twelve

Gus, Moon Man, and I sat at at the tree trunk table near the bar at the Soggy Dollar, and I was busily contemplating what the next thirty years in a Cuban prison might be like.

"Cuba," I said, between sips of my Painkiller. "We're royally screwed, now, or Chester is. Or most likely all of us, if things work out the way they usually do."

"What'daya mean?" said Gus, drinking his own straight Pusser's rum.

"What'daya mean, What'daya mean? I mean how the hell are we supposed to get into Cuba?" I said.

"By getting in the plane and flying there," said Gus.

"Yeah, right; what, are you a treetop flier, too?" I said. "I don't think I want to try sneaking under communist radar."

"So we just putt up to the dock, instead," said Gus.

"And get shot," I said. "Been there, done that, almost tried it again today, rather look for a new experience for once."

"You're one of those people who think we're not allowed to travel to Cuba, aren't you? That Castro or one of his brothers is standing in a tower with a pair of binoculars waiting for an American to put a toe on their island," said Gus.

"Kind of like you and me looking for each other," I said. "And yeah, that's how it is...isn't it?"

"Not really," said Gus. "We can go into the country any time we want. The good old United States says it's pretty much illegal, especially without a lot of tour guided crap, but Cuba doesn't mind if we come. And it helps I have a commercial pilot's license."

"He's right, man," said Moon Man. He took a long pull on the straw of his virgin Pina Colada. "Just don't write home to Uncle Sam about it."

"I didn't plan to; the two of us haven't been pen pals for some time," I said. "And do you ever take those sunglasses off, Moon Mon? It's night, for crying out loud. I don't see how you even can walk."

Moon Man adjusted his little circular, Lennon style shades. "I see with my-"

"Yeah, yeah; I forgot about the other eye. Still, it would be nice to see your first two eyes," I said.

"Thanks, but my shades are prescription, too," said Moon Man. "If I took them off, then I really wouldn't be able to see where I was going."

So it turned out Moon Mon had a practical side like the rest of us, after all. "Finally, something about you that makes sense," I said. "But back to the Cuban

Chester Crisis; you guys are serious, and sure. We can just fly there, and we'll be fine?"

"We should be," said Gus.

"Yeah, as long as they're being cool, there. Of course, Cuba is still an authoritarian state that routinely employs repressive methods against internal dissent and monitors and responds to perceived threats to its authority," said Moon Man. "I memorized it from the United States government's travel page."

"Well, let's try not to do anything while we're there they might perceive as a threat to their authority," I said. "I don't feel like experiencing any repressive methods."

"Ditto," said Gus. "But I've never had any problems in the past."

"You've been there before?" I said.

"Yeah, a few times," said Gus. "Okay, maybe about twenty; best Mojitos in the world."

"Do you just fly around from place to place looking for good drinks?" I said.

"More or less," said Gus. "Is there something wrong with that?"

I tried to come up with an angle that would make Gus' lifestyle look bad, but found I couldn't do so without bringing my own down. "I guess not," I said. "It seems like there should be, but I'm too messed up myself to know what it is. Do you ever get the idea there's something wrong with us?"

"With me, no," said Gus, finishing off his rum with a long gulp, as if to put an exclamation point on his statement. "With you, more than I can say."

"Hola, my friends!" said a friendly, familiar voice, as someone patted me on the back before I could grumble about Gus' proclamation.

"Jolly Roger!" I said, then turned on my seat at the table to be sure of my identification, since I didn't have any of Cuba's surveillance gear. "What are you doing here?"

"I've started staying on Jost three times a week this time of year so dat my ferry goes from here to di island, den back to Jost, and den back to di island again one day, den from di island to Jost, den back to di island, and den back to Jost again di next," said Roger.

I tried to follow exactly what the hell he meant, but started getting seasick on the ride back and forth. "I'll take your word for it," I said. "Sit down and join us."

"I'll do dat," said Roger. "I'm dying to know how di us part happened."

"You mean, him and me sitting here together?" said Gus, while getting up to head to the bar to get another round of drinks. "We have a shaky truce in place right now; it's nothing permanent, I assure you. I'll let him explain it."

"Dis should be good," said Roger, sitting down next to me.

"Well, you see..." I said, trying to figure out the shortest way to tell the story. "Oh, forget it. It's too nice a night to recap the whole thing. Let's just say we're still on the trail to find Chester, and our paths crossed and converged. Gus and I might not get along, but both of us want to find him, so..."

"...and? You sounded like you were gonna say someting else, too, Captain Harry," said Roger.

"...so evidently we're going to Cuba together," I said. "And now that I think about it, I'm wondering how the hell that suddenly happened. Seems like only yesterday I was saying how I had nothing to do and I was standing on shore keeping Gus from setting foot on my island, and now I'm going to an authoritarian state with him."

"An authoritarian state that routinely employs repressive methods against internal dissent and monitors and responds to perceived threats to its authority," said Moon Man. "And it was yesterday, wasn't it?"

"Yeah, at least I think so. Though I could have sworn time flies when you're having rum," I said, while further killing the pain I didn't feel with another gulp of Painkiller pineapple coconut.

"Maybe you haven't been having enough of di rum," said Roger.

"Here's more," said Gus, handing out a fresh round. "Why don't we move down by the water with it, though; I just looked and there's some chairs open."

"I'm game," I said. "I am a son of di beach, after all."

"You'll get no argument from me on that," said Gus.

I picked up my flip-flops from under the table, and we walked across the sand towards the shore. My footwear pretty much kept the same schedule as I did; when I relaxed, they did, too. If I was sitting they were generally off my feet, lounging around. I sometimes wondered why I bothered with them at all, until I'd try to walk across one of our dirt roads on Paradiso and my paws reminded me what pansies they were whenever they encountered the tiniest of rocks. And besides, they were flip-flops, and I simply had to have a pair at all times.

I turned my chosen chair towards the ocean and plopped down in it with an audible ahh. I'd never understood why we say ahh when we sat; I got the drinking ahh thing, but what the mouth has to do with your buttocks being happy is beyond me. I guess maybe we're just pushing air out of our bodies, but the reason I've chosen to believe is that it's the human version of a purr; when you think about it, we seem to ahh when we're suddenly feeling very contented, or doing something that's putting us on the road to it.

And sitting on the beach at night always made me feel ahhfully good, and it did so again now. During the day the ocean was big, bold, and beautiful, but at night, it always seemed more subdued, and mysterious. In some ways the lady was even more seductive, as if she'd gone from a sunkissed, perky, statuesque blonde to a smoldering, inscrutable brunette. During the day the waters made me want to just jump right in without thinking, but at night, I always wondered what might lie below that dark, glassy surface. And as I've said, I love a good mystery.

"I've been meaning to ask you about Chester," said Moon Man. "Gus said he saved your life twice? What happened, man?"

"Oh; that," I said. "Yes, he did, although some people might not count the first time. A few years before I actually did leave everything in my old life behind and run away to the Caribbean, I was on a business trip in Miami; big dry cleaning convention. I know it's hard to believe, but that got pretty boring in a hurry, so I decided to skip the last few days, rent a car, go exploring, and have some fun. Well, by the time I was through with South Beach, Key Largo, and Islamorada, I was planning to go home, pack my things, and come right back down there for good. I was having just way too much fun to let it end, and I'd gotten into another big fight with my wife just before I'd left on my trip. But then I stumbled into Crazy Chester's Bar and Boat Stop just north of Key West for a bite to eat, and in spite of the fact that he himself had left his life behind in Chicago, he talked me into going back home to my family."

"So like Jack, you knew Chester before you even came to di island and Paradiso Shores," said Moon Man.

"Yeah, I did," I said. "I was pretty surprised, and happy, when I ran into him on di island."

"And you consider him talking you out of leaving di states the first time a good ting, den?" said Roger. "I'm just curious; why was it so different from when you eventually did come down here to stay, mon?"

"I wasn't ready, and he told me so," I said. "I might have been having a blast partying my rear end off, but while things at home were a little rough at the time, we still had our good moments, too. And he said it wasn't enough to be running away to something, you had to be running away *from* something as well."

119

"Never heard that one before," said Gus. "Everyone always told me you shouldn't run away from your problems, period. Not that I listened, of course."

"He just meant it works both ways. You shouldn't run away unless you have something worth running to, and you shouldn't run to something unless what you're running away from is really that bad," I said. "I'm not good at putting it into words, but he managed to do it, and it made sense. And the way I look at it, he saved my life. I have some good memories of those last two years I had at home, and if I would have come down here at the time I might have always regretted leaving, and that would have screwed up every year I've had since."

"Don't you ever regret it anyway? Leaving your family behind, all that?" said Gus. "I never had one, so it was no big deal for me, but..."

"No, I don't," I said. "Sure, I wish maybe things had worked out differently, but it is what it is. I probably could have worked a little harder at making the home life work, but when you get to a certain point, it's pretty hard to change things. Once it starts to go downhill, about all you can do is hold it in place; you have so much that's happened, so much baggage to carry, that it's damned difficult to push your life back uphill. Anyway, I don't really want to talk about it, but

120

that's how I consider Chester saving my life the first time. And by the way, it's a good thing I never made it all the way down to Key West that trip, because I'm not sure any amount of Chester's wisdom could have talked me out of it after that."

"Dat be true," said Jolly Roger.

"And the second time he saved you?" asked Moon Man.

"The very next day he took me out fishing on the Lazy Lizard, and like an idiot, I decided to jump in the ocean. While the boat was moving, no less, and at a pretty good clip. It was hot, and it just looked so inviting, and I'd been slurping down the Chesteritas he'd been making on his frozen concoction maker. I'm guessing I was pretty dehydrated from the last few days of fun, because my leg cramped up something fierce. And by the time he'd turned the boat around to go back and get my stupid ass, I'd gone under. My last thoughts were I figured I was done for, but I woke up back on the Lazy Lizard, spitting sea water. Chester had, pulled me back out and given me CPR. Not that I deserved it."

"Yeah, I'd say you owe him on dat one," said Roger.

"Enough to go to Cuba to find him, evidently," I said. "Maybe we can lead a revolution while we're there, too."

"I haven't been listening to the news lately, say for about twenty years," said Gus. "But knowing Chester, he may have already started one."

"Well, if we arrive and everyone is running around the country without shirts and shoes, that might be the first clue Chester's been forcing social reforms," I said.

"Even di women?" said Roger.

"We can hope," I said.

"Hmm; maybe I'll get someone to cover my shuttle runs for a few days and go wit you," said Roger, thoughtfully.

"Viva la revolucion!" I said, hoisting my Painkiller in the air.

Chapter Thirteen

"And I say di mango is di perfect fruit," said Keyon.

"Yes, I heard ya; again and again. But what I want to know is how many coconuts fell on your head dis week?" said Kian. "Because everyone knows di banana is by far di best."

"I prefer papayas, myself," said Maggie.

"Careful; you don't want to get caught in the crossfire," I said. "Besides, this is a private argument. Go get your own."

"Just trying to change things up a bit," said Mags.

"I tried that once myself, and the discussion ended up lasting for a month," I said. "Let's just keep it between those two, because three sided debates never end."

It was breakfast again at the Rumwreck and I was back on Paradiso Shores, waiting for Gus to fly in and pick me up. I'd flown my own plane home from the BVI this morning since we were going to take Gus' to Cuba (not my ideal situation, but like Gus said, he had the commercial license). I knew I'd feel better about it sitting there waiting for me instead of on Jost for the next however many years, if our rescue mission turned sour. And it gave me one last chance to see my little wreck of a plot of paradise, and a last good meal in case I ended up in front of a firing squad. Which seemed likely, given my tendency to have guns pointed at me.

I still wasn't convinced we weren't about to get ourselves into a whole mess of trouble, no matter what Gus and Moon Man said. Although I had to admit, I did feel a little better hearing what Mags had had to say on the matter. She at least had some common sense, compared to Major Tom and Levi Grizwood, so when she told me we should be fine, I believed her. It was just that word *should* in there that bothered me, since I often seemed to end up in the skinny slice of the Key Lime pie chart of possible outcomes.

But it didn't matter, since I was going, no matter what. Moon Man had decided to stay behind back on di island, however, taking Jolly Roger's shuttle home. He'd suddenly remembered something about some incident during his travels in the sixties involving a balcony, a bag of rotting turnips, El Presidente's daughters, and an open convertible in the motorcade. He was sure Fidel would have forgotten by now, but felt we'd be safer if he didn't take any chances. I tended to agree; not because of the turnips, but because he was Moon Man, and not having him tag along made me feel safer immediately, since we'd have a far better chance of being inconspicuous.

He did feel his karma had been repaired by his small part in Operation Free the Chester. I wasn't sure exactly what he'd done, but I guess pointing me in the right direction to begin with had been pretty helpful. And maybe he'd somehow served as a sort of buffer between Gus and I. It was going to be interesting to see how we were going to get along now that there would only be the two of us, and I had a sneaking suspicion this was all an elaborate plot concocted by Gus to get me to Cuba and leave me there. Probably payback for locking him in that porta-potty on the Wind Song Resort construction site a few years back.

"Don't you tink you should get going?" said the fisherman.

"What do you want me to do; swim to Cuba? Or should I take my boat, so we're attacking with di island air force and the Paradiso Shores navy?" I said. "I told you, Gus is coming to pick me up. Then I'm going."

"I can't believe you're actually getting into a plane with Gus," said Maggie.

"I know, and for the third time in two days," I said. "And I'm not drunk *this* time, either. Although maybe if I hurry..."

"Hey, we're tryin' to have an argument here," said Keyon.

"Yes, but I'm sorry, it's a pretty weak one this morning," I said.

125

"Ya, I know, mon," said Kian, a bit solemnly for him. "I guess our hearts just aren't into it today."

"I'll be fine; don't worry," I said.

"I was tinking of Chester," said Kian.

"Me too, sitting on di floor in dat jail cell on di straw," said Keyon.

"Why doesn't anybody ever anguish over me?" I said.

"Besides di fact dat you're di son of di beach?" said the fisherman.

"Yeah, besides that," I said.

"I promise to try and feel a twinge or two while you're gone," said Maggie.

"Thanks, Mags," I said.

"But not if you call me that again," she said, picking up a strawberry out of the bowl and throwing it at me. It bounced off my chest and landed on the table, and Starch happily waddled over, picked it up, and started eating it.

"Do you want my half of the bar if I don't make it back, Maggie?" I said.

"Really?" said Mags. "You mean it?"

"Sure," I said.

"If you're serious, then, no, I don't," she said, taking a sip of coffee. "What would I want with this dump? Although at least I'd get along with the fisherman better than you. Wouldn't I, hot-stuff?" she said, with a little wink at the fisherman.

"Yes, maam!" grinned the fisherman, who'd always had a thing for Maggie.

"We'll take di bar, Captain," said Kian.

I shrugged. "Fine by me; you two can each have half of my half," I said.

"We gonna be partners, Keyon!" said Kian.

"Cool, brother!" said Keyon, as the two gave each other a high five.

"Just try not to be too upset if I actually make it home," I said.

"We'll be almost as happy, I promise," said Kian.

"Yeah, almost," said Keyon.

"I can just feel all that island love," I said. My ears thought they heard something, and I focused them (funny how you can do that) and made out the sound of a plane in the far distance. "That would be Gus, I guess. I better grab my stuff."

"It's already down on di dock, Captain," said Keyon.

"Not in a hurry to get rid of me, are you?" I said, standing up.

"We wanted to get to work on di roof," said Kian. "We are gonna fix it up and surprise you."

"You idiot; how can it be a surprise now?" said Keyon.

"Maybe he won't come back," said Kian.

"It still wouldn't be a surprise, den," said Keyon. "Him would be sitting on di straw on di floor in di jail cell, and thinkin' about how nice his roof must be by now."

"Yeah, I guess you be right," said Kian.

"I'm coming back!" I growled, then sighed and looked around. My ocean was still there, next to my beach where it belonged. And my palm trees swayed a bit in the gentle breeze coming off the water, making little rustling noises. And my bar; that worn, beaten, weathered, and dilapidated eyesore, was still there, too, looking to my eyes like a sight that rivaled the Taj Mahal for beauty.

"Thanks for the thought, guys, but don't you dare touch that roof; I want it to be just like it is now when I get home," I said. "It wouldn't be the Wreck if it wasn't about to fall over."

"Dat's okay, too," said Keyon. "We're both pretty good at not doing something."

"Dat's for sure," said the fisherman.

I gave Starch a quick scratch on his beak where he liked it, said, "Adios, amigos," to everyone else, then walked over by the dock.

I was standing in the sand, facing the water and watching Gus come in for a landing, wondering if this would be the time I'd get to see him crash, when I felt a tap on my shoulder. I turned and found Maggie there, and to my surprise she gave me a big hug, then turned and walked away.

I watched her go for a moment, then turned back to Mother Ocean.

"Now I'm really worried," I thought to myself.

Chapter Fourteen

Gus was saying something in Spanish into the airplane radio, and it made me wish I'd learned a second language, since it sounded suspiciously like, "I have him; prepare the interrogation room". Then again, for all I knew, he was pre-ordering us a round of Mojitos to be delivered to the docks, or six trained welcoming flamingos performing a Gloria Estefan medley. Such was my knowledge of Spanish.

I found no snappily dressed waiters with trays of minty drinks or flamingos singing *"the rhythm is gonna get you"* on the docks as we disembarked, however. And after a reasonably long but torture free session with immigration, we stood in the streets of Matanzas.

It was like stepping back into my childhood. At least it would have been, if I'd been born earlier, and in a Latin country. As it was, it felt like I was on some period movie set, surrounded by classic American cars from the fifties. Some looked like they were about to fall down and die right were they were, sort of like the Rumwreck, but most were in amazingly good condition. It was like heaven. To me, for the most part, modern cars just don't have any style, and the ones that do tend to copy older models. But everywhere I looked now, I'd see a white fifty-eight Buick Limited with the

Fashion-Aire Dynastar Grill, a blue fifty-seven finned out Cadillac Eldorado, or a red nineteen fifty-one Dodge Wayfarer Sportabout roadster convertible. I was like a kid in a toy store; *"I want that, I want that, I want that, I want that."* And I definitely had to have one of those.

"What's with all these old cars, Gus?" I finally had to ask. "Do they just live for style here?"

"They don't have any choice; they're only allowed to buy and sell the cars that were around when Fidel took over," said Gus.

"Really?" I said. "How about that; regulated coolness."

"I don't think that's what he had in mind," said Gus. "But yeah, it is scenic, isn't it?"

"That's for sure," I said. "So what's the plan?"

"Mojitos," said Gus.

"I figured that, knowing you, but shouldn't we be looking for Chester, too?" I said.

"We will be. I don't have a clue where to start, however, and I'm guessing you don't, either. But my favorite cantina is a great spot for information," said Gus.

"So you've been here, too; to this city, I mean," I said.

"Yeah, here and Havana, just up the coast to the west. And by the way, if you head dead north," he said turning in that direction and pointing across the ocean, "that way, and go about a hundred or so miles, you run smack dab into Chester's old place in the Keys. I used to fly that route all the time; easy to navigate. That's how I found this city in the first place, just heading south from Chester's Bar and Boat Stop."

"Don't you think that's a bit odd, that he gets kidnapped and ends up on almost the exact same longitude line as his old bar?" I said.

"Not for Chester," said Gus. "Come on; let's grab a taxi and get a room at the inn, and then we'll see what we can see."

About an hour later we were sitting at a table with a colorful umbrella on a stone patio overlooking the ocean, a round of Mojitos in front of us. I picked mine up and looked at it, a glass of frosty lime and mint surrounded by silver rum goodness, definitely one of the most eye pleasing cocktails of all time. I took a sip, and it tastily lived up to its outer facade, as well.

I was currently suffering from a case of aesthetic overload. Matanzas was a beautiful old city, the old being in the same way as Key West or the French Quarter of New Orleans. Like modern cars, modern buildings don't always have much going for them in the way of charm. Maybe in fifty years we'll develop a sense of nostalgia for the new ones, too, and feel all warm and fuzzy when we see a bank built in two thousand and twelve, but I highly doubt it. I would never want to be called quaint, but if I was a building, I could definitely live with it, and might even prefer it. Or, for that matter, if I was a city.

Of course, it didn't hurt that Matanzas was on a Caribbean island, and that it was built with a Latin flair. And that we were siting next to the waters of the Atlantic with Mojitos in front of us as a Cuban musical trio sang about, well, I had no idea what they were singing about, since I didn't understand the language. But that just made it all the more exotic.

"I gotta hand it to Chester; if I was going to be kidnapped to some supposedly evil country, this doesn't seem like such a bad place to be dragged to," I said.

"Not as bad as people make it out to be, is it?" said Gus. "Although it can get pretty ugly, too, if you get out of line, or even look like you're getting out of line."

"People seem pretty content, though, from what I can tell," I said.

"Humans are really good at finding a level to be happy at," said Gus. "In a way, that's the funny thing about total freedom. It seems like it just gives people more to bitch about."

133

"It's like spoiling a kid; the more they have, the more they think they're owed. We have it pretty good back in the States, but it's never enough, and so many people are miserable," I said. "I guess here and places like it in the Caribbean, you're only going to have so much and once you accept that, you stop moaning about it. What's that line from that Sheryl Crow song? It's not having what you want, it's wanting what you've got?"

"Well, I've got my Mojito, so I want what I've got, and I'm good," said Gus, taking a drink. "And by the way, it's we *had* it pretty good back in the states for me and you."

"Same difference," I said. "So why do you suppose you and I are able to sit here and talk without being tempted to throw a punch at one another, but not back at home?"

"The night is young," said Gus. "But it's probably because we're not around our friends. I'm the pilot, and I'm the grizzly one in the group; I don't like there being two of us, like we're a club or something. Out here, we don't have a group, so it doesn't matter so much."

"That's pretty childish, don't you think?" I said.

"Damned right it is, and proud of it," said Gus.

"Cheers to that," I said, and I held out my Mojito and we clinked glasses.

"Hola, Meester Grizwood!" said a Cuban looking gent who'd walked up next to our table.

"Alvaro!" said Gus. "I was hoping you'd show up, hombre. Have a seat."

"What brings you to my country today, my friend?" said Alvaro, while sitting down and taking off his straw cowboy hat. "Are you here for business or pleasure? And who ees this with you?"

"Everything I do is for pleasure; I thought you knew that by now," said Gus. "And this is my...what the hell are you, anyway?"

I thought about it for a moment, then said, "Accomplice, collaborator, and accessory, come to mind."

"Let's skip the accessory part; makes you sound like a purse. Although having you here does make me look good," said Gus.

"Only because you're in my shadow, and you look better in the dark," I said.

Maybe Gus was right; the minute someone else showed up, the digs between us started in again.

I stuck my hand out to Alvaro before Gus could retort, and said, "Nice to meet you. I'm Captain Harry."

"He says with a straight face," said Gus.

"Does, *"Nice to meet you. I'm Harry,"* sound better?" I said.

"Ya gotta point," said Gus. "Alvaro here knows everything about everything in these parts. If anyone is gonna know something about Chester's whereabouts, it's him."

"Then you are here looking for someone?" said Alvaro. "Tell me about it."

"As far as we know, a friend of ours, they call him Crazy Chester, was taken here from Jost Van Dyke by some minor bad guy," said Gus. "What was his name again?"

I leafed through the pile of notes in my head, then said, "Luis. Is that really all we know? Now that I think about it, there must be thousands of Luis' here. But that's all the Fox told us; that and Luis had a hacienda outside of town."

"Maybe we should have threatened him a while longer," said Gus.

"It's because we're amateurs at this; next time we'll bring Black Dog along," I said.

"I think I may know who you mean, though," said Alvaro, stroking his mustache. "There ees a man; a family, really, who lives just outside of town in a beautiful hacienda on a hill. They have strong ties to the government, and pretty much do as they please, meaning they make a lot of pesos from shady dealings I don't even want to talk about. I know the youngest

136

son does leave the country often to go to the islands where he does...business. And his name ees Luis."

"Sounds like our man," said Gus. "How do we get in there?"

"Into the hacienda?" said Alvaro, somewhat incredulously.

"Yes. We think Chester is being held there, so we need to get inside and take a look around for him," I said.

"You can't. I've been to the property, and there ees no way in if they don't want you in," said Alvaro.

"Alvaro drives a delivery truck; gets him into all sorts of places," said Gus. "But there is no can't, Alvaro; anything is doable, if you need to do it badly enough."

"There ees a tall fence around the property, and guards with guns and dogs walk the perimeter," said Alvaro. "And they have cameras all over the place."

"Guns and dogs? Maybe there is a can't after all. Chester, it was nice knowing ya," said Gus, raising his glass to him in a toast.

"Let's not give up so easy; Jason Bourne would find a way in," I said.

"Last time I checked, neither of us was a trained operative," said Gus. "Except maybe in the not so covert art of drinking."

"Look at that sunset out there," I said, pointing at Sol as he slowly sank into the horizon, sending a dazzling array of pastel colors across the sky. "Now can you tell me, looking at that, that there's something that can't be done?"

"Yeah, I already said it once, and gazing all dewy eyed at the sky isn't gonna change anything," said Gus. "I'm sorry, but I don't feel like getting my ass shot or chewed off."

"I don't either; once was enough," I said. "But maybe we haven't thought of all our options, yet. If Alvaro got in with his delivery truck, for example, maybe we could hide inside and get in that way."

"I quit last week and became a bartender," said Alvaro. "More money, less work."

"See? I told you," said Gus. "It's hopeless. Might as well just sit here and drink, instead," and he waved at the waitress, giving her the international sign for another round.

"That's it? You're gonna give up, leave our friend to his fate, and sit here downing Mojitos?" I said. "I always knew you were a wuss."

"No, that's not all I'm gonna do," said Gus.

"No?" I said.

"No. I'm gonna dance, too," said Gus, wiggling around in his seat to the salsa beat. "These are bad men; we're not. We're drinkers, eaters, dancers, lovers, and nappers. We just don't have the right skill set for the job."

"Look, Chester's in that hacienda, or at the very least, he was in there," I said. "And we're gonna find a way in, even if we have to walk right up and knock on the damned front door."

And the next morning, that's precisely what we did.

After a full night of drinking, eating, dancing, and napping, having not quite managing the loving as usual, of course.

Chapter Fifteen

It wasn't the front door we ended up knocking on, since we couldn't reach it, but the buzzer button at the front gate. Alvaro had dropped us off down the hill and out of sight (in an orange and white fifty-three Ford Crestline Victoria, which I never wanted to get out of), not wanting to come any closer to the Moreno estate.

Gus and I had walked the rest of the way, then watched from a small grove of trees until the two guards near the gate had wandered a ways off, not being in a rush to be confronted by them, though it seemed inevitable. Which it was, since they came running over when we hit the call button, as if its sole purpose in life was to summon them back.

"What do you want?" said the guards and a voice over the intercom, at almost the same time. I wasn't sure who to answer, but since the guards had the guns, I elected to address them first and hope the voice would hear it as well.

"We're here to see Luis," I said.

"Nobody just walks up and sees Luis," said one of the men from behind the gate, dressed in your typical movie guard attire of a black suit and tie, white shirt, and dark sunglasses. If he and his partner had suddenly traded places, I would have been hard pressed to notice.

"Luis must get lonely, then," I said. "Don't you guys at least have Jehovah's Witnesses around here to talk to?"

"We just need to speak to him for a moment," said Gus.

"What you need has nothing to do with it," said the other man in black. "Now go away before you regret it."

"I already regret it; it's damned hot and I'm hungover, thanks to him," I said, pointing at Gus. "I'd like to get this over with as quickly as possible, so if one of you two morons would open the gate, we can go inside and get out of your hair."

The two men looked at one another, as if not used to being spoken to in such a manner. I wasn't used to speaking to men with sub-machine guns in such a manner either, so it was new territory for everyone involved.

"What do these men look like?" said the voice over the intercom, which made me wonder if Alvaro had been right about there being cameras on the property.

"Just a couple of old American gringos," said one of the guards.

"Old?" said Gus and I, at the same time. "I'm not old," I added, going solo. "Vintage, maybe, but old, never."

"Shoot them," said the voice.

"And we're not American, either," said Gus. "Not exactly, anyway."

"I don't think they're listening," I said, as the two men pointed their guns at us. "Got any ideas?"

"Yeah, but since we went ahead and came here anyway like you insisted, it's a little late now," said Gus. "I don't know who was stupider; you with your idiotic plan, or me, for going along with it."

"I'd say you, but then I knew that before any of this happened," I said, determined to get the last insult in between us if we were about to die. "The least they could do is tell us what happened to Chester; I'm gonna hate going to heaven without knowing the end of the mystery."

"You don't have to worry; I doubt you'll be heading in that direction anyway," said Gus.

"Like you will," I said.

"Heaven forbid," said Gus. "Literally."

"Wait a minute," said the voice. "Did one of these gringos just mention Chester?"

"Si," said one of the guards, obviously disappointed at being stopped before he could fire his gun, which I'm sure was the reason he took the job in the first place.

"Ask them what about Chester," said the voice.

"What about-" started one of the guards.

"We heard him; we're standing right here too, you know," I said. "Chester is a friend of ours. We heard a man named Luis brought him to Cuba, and that we could find that man here. We just want to find out what happened."

"Why didn't you say so in the first place?" said the voice, and the gate suddenly clicked and swung open. "Escort them up to the house."

"Uh...thanks," I said, into the intercom.

One of the guards pointed with his gun down the driveway leading inwards away from the gate, as if we might wander off somewhere else instead, and Gus and I began walking down it, the man following closely behind.

"So what do you think that was all about?" Gus leaned over and asked.

"You mean, letting us in all of a sudden?" I said. "I don't know, but for some reason, it doesn't make me feel any better."

"Maybe because before we were outside the gate and could at least try to run away, no matter how useless it might have been. And now we're locked inside," said Gus.

"Yeah, it does give it a sense of finality, doesn't it? Nice place, though," I said, looking around as we walked. "Makes me want to start a life of crime."

Call it a hacienda or an estate; it didn't matter, it was beautiful either way. The path we were walking on was done entirely in red brick, with lights all along its length. Green trees of every sort grew abundantly above the perfectly manicured lawn, landscaped with stones and flowers. And when the house itself came into view, it turned out to be a two story sprawling mansion, roman arches and pillars everywhere, built with white stone and topped by classic red clay roof tiles. I wasn't sure if we were being taken to see Luis, or Augustus Caesar.

"In communism, isn't everyone in the country supposed to own everything together?" I said, as we walked past a red Ferrari parked on the driveway, which wrapped around a huge fountain. It was one of the very few newer cars I'd seen since my arrival in the country.

"Or own nothing together," said Gus. "I can't remember which."

"Maybe it's socialism I'm thinking of," I said. "Anyway, these guys would be doing well by U.S. standards."

"But do they get American Idol?" said Gus.

I pointed up at the giant satellite dish perched on top of the roof.

"Never mind," said Gus.

"Obviously they've found a loophole in the system," I said.

"I think it's called the *"crime pays"* exception," said Gus.

We were led inside the house by our guide, down a long hallway with an Italian marble floor lined with art and vases. At least I figured the floor was Italian, though it didn't speak, so I couldn't tell for sure if it had a pisano accent. Eventually we were put in a room that I guess you'd call a solarium, especially if you had so many rooms, as Luis obviously did, that you had to have a lot of different names for them so you could tell the waitstaff where you wanted to have your breakfast.

"Wait here, and don't touch anything," said the guard gruffly, and he left the room and closed the door behind him.

"He could learn a thing or two from Tour Guide Barbie," I said.

"What should we do now?" said Gus.

I looked around. "Wait here, and don't touch anything," I said. "Except I think my ass is gonna touch that chair." And I walked over and sat down at a table near the window.

Gus did the same, and we waited quietly for Luis to arrive.

This Luis did seem to have the life. I had one, too, and I loved it, but I was guessing that he didn't exactly bemoan his fate every day when he got out of bed, either. Power and wealth did have their advantages; it was just the spending your life trying and failing to get the two that dragged most people down. It was all well and good to be part of the elite class, but most of us were never going to make the cut because, well, it's elite. Better to just find some simple thing you love and shoot for spending as much of your life as you can doing it, instead. Like lounging around on a rustic, sandy beach in front of a rundown bar all day.

That didn't mean I wasn't currently enjoying sitting in this lovely, sunny room with the central air. I was enjoying it so much in fact, that by the time somebody showed up I was nodding off in the coolness, my hat brim pulled low to block out the sunniness. I was still feeling the effects of the night before, and recovery was slow from what had turned into pitchers of Mojitos and enough dancing to wear my vintage bones fully out. It wasn't until Gus kicked me under the table that I finally realized we were no longer alone in the room.

"I see you have made yourselves comfortable," said the impeccably groomed, middle aged, Latin gentleman, who was dressed in a casual, but expensive looking shirt and white shorts.

"Well, I figured if anyone was going to consider shooting us again, I wanted to be rested enough so I could enjoy it this time," I said, sitting up in my chair.

"My apologies for that," said the man. "I should have inquired as to what you were doing here before considering killing you."

"That would be the polite thing to do," I said. "But as they say back on di island, no problem, mon. You must be Luis?"

"Actually, Luis is my son," said the man. "My name is Rafael."

"We really needed to speak to Luis," said Gus.

"My son isn't here, but I can assure you, I know all about the situation," said Rafael. "But let's not speak here. Are you hungry? I've ordered breakfast to be brought to the patio by the pool."

Just as I'd thought; there were probably seventeen patios, and this one was designated as the *"by the pool"* one. "I don't suppose we can just sit here where it's cool, can we? I'm still engaged in recovery efforts from some of your Cuban hospitality last night."

"I prefer to spend as much of my time outside as possible," said Rafael; something I could relate to, at least. "But perhaps a Bloody Mary or two might help with your rehabilitation?"

"Now you're talking," I said, while standing up, now that I had the motivation to do so. "Lead the way, jefe."

Chapter Sixteen

An hour later I was well fed, lubricated, and refurbished, putting the wraps on my third Bloody Mary, having thoroughly enjoyed all sorts of Cuban breakfast treats I hadn't formerly been acquainted with but now couldn't wait to get intimate with again. I'd been sorely tempted to jump in the nearby, extremely inviting looking pool as well, or to casually fall into it so as to not seem too presumptuous to our new host. But the food had kept me busy up until now, and now that the now had arrived, I found myself way too content and stuffed to fall into anything, except for perhaps a hammock for a good long nap.

Rafael had refused to talk about Chester and Luis until breakfast was finished, except to assure us that he was alive and well; he said that it came too close to constituting business, which he never discussed during a meal, as to not spoil it. I could appreciate the sentiment; I never discussed business while I ate, either. Then again, I didn't have any business to discuss, unless you wanted to count arguing with the fisherman about what color drink straws we should use next.

Finally a servant cleared the last of the dishes away while another passed out a round of Mimosas, and when the two had disappeared, Rafael said, "Now we can talk. I'm sure you're very curious what has become of your friend, and I respect your bravery for coming to my estate to find him. Especially since I assume you know who I am?"

"Just generalities," I said. "We know you're an..." and I searched for the right word, "important man around here."

"I'm a tyrant," said Rafael. "At least that's what some of the people would say. The others would say I provide the people with the things they can't acquire somewhere else."

"So what does Chester have to do with any of that?" said Gus, who'd been extremely quiet since we'd arrived. I couldn't tell if it was because he was a little frightened or, like me, a lot hungover. Or maybe he just didn't have anything to say.

"Nothing; your friend has nothing to do with what we do," said Rafael.

"Then how did he end up here?" I said. "Why did Luis bring him to Cuba?"

"It's a bit of a long story," said Rafael. "You know that Chester came to see my son, Luis, on Jost Van Dyke. He wanted to buy an emerald for a ring for his girlfriend."

"For Akiko, yes," I said. "I figured something went wrong with the sale, although I couldn't see how

Chester could have caused any trouble, knowing him like we do."

"And he didn't. And nothing went wrong, either. Luis didn't have any emeralds in his stock on Jost, but there were some elsewhere. And he told Chester he would have one of our men deliver one to him," said Rafael.

"Wow; a shady dealer who delivers," I said. "No offense."

"None taken; we are what we are," said Rafael. "Anyway, our men are constantly going back and forth around the Caribbean, so it wasn't going to be a problem bringing the stone to him. But Chester said he preferred to have it brought not to di island itself so it wouldn't spoil the surprise, but to a small neighboring island called Isla De Luis. A place my son had never heard of before."

"Yeah, it's not called that on any maps; probably too small to even have an official title," said Gus. "We named it after an old friend."

"And that's what drew my son's interest. They got to talking; my son said Luis was his name, too, and Chester told him about your friend Luis, and that's when my son decided to bring him back here."

"Uh, timeout. At that point, did Chester want to go? He was already running late for getting home and opening his bar," I said.

"I don't know, but I'm fairly sure he wasn't forced to come," said Rafael. "He seemed happy to help when he got here."

"That sounds like Chester," I said. "And now we're coming to the part where you tell me *why* he came here to begin with?"

"Si," said Rafael. "My son was named after his uncle, Luis. My father, Alejandro's, brother. That Luis left Cuba when he was young, sent to America by my grandparents to learn modern business and chemistry. Then things changed here in my country, and he was unable to return, or didn't wish to. My family lost the rum company they had owned for generations, taken away by the government."

"And our Luis from di island was your father's brother?" I said. "Wow; I may need another Mimosa or three."

"We had learned through letters that Luis was furious at what had happened to my family, and rightfully so. He wanted nothing more to do with Cuba," said Rafael. "But my father, Alejandro, took a different approach. He embraced the government, choosing to be friends with those in power, helping them however he could, so they might help him in return one day. It paid off, and he was able to build his own small empire."

"And how did Luis take that?" asked Gus.

"Not well; Luis cut off all ties with my father, as did the rest of my family. Years and years went by, and they never spoke, and my papa didn't even know what had become of his brother. But as my father grew old, and came towards the end of his life, he started to regret the things he had done, especially losing the connection with Luis. He thought his brother was still somewhere in America, and he sent people searching for him, but to no avail. Although he did learn through one of our other relatives in the states that Luis had eventually returned to somewhere in the Caribbean. And then finally my son ran into Chester, just a few days ago," said Rafael.

"What made him think it might be the same Luis? There must be thousands of Luis' throughout the islands," I said.

"Just the things Chester had told him. About Luis being the master blender for di island Rum Company, and the approximate time period in which he had left Cuba," said Rafael. "It made the odds seem pretty strong that he was the same man."

"So your son brought Chester here to talk to you?" said Gus.

"To talk to my father," said Rafael.

"Wait a minute; your father, Alejandro, is still alive?" I said. "The way you said your father was near the end of his life..."

153

"He passed away three days ago," said Rafael. "The morning after Chester left us. We buried him in the family cemetery just yesterday."

"I'm sorry," I said. "No wonder you wanted to shoot me."

"It was his time; and he learned what he had wanted to learn. It would have been better if he'd found Luis had still been alive and could have talked to him, but he knew at least that his brother's life had been a good lone, and that he had died happy," said Rafael. "My father was able to pass in peace, and I think that was all he was hanging on for, to find out what happened to Luis."

"Not anywhere near any of the reasons I had for Chester being here," said Gus. "You, Harry?"

"Not even close," I said. "So where is Chester now?"

"He should be back at home," said Rafael.

"But he's not," I said.

Rafael looked puzzled. "I don't understand. Chester was here for two days, telling my father everything he knew. He was treated as an honored guest, and by the time he left, we were all friends, I think. Although he still stubbornly refused to wear any of the fine shirts we laid out for him."

"Don't feel bad; I'm not sure you could make him do that at gunpoint," said Gus.

"I told Luis to have someone take him home to di island, by boat. He should have been back," and Rafael did some figuring, "about four days ago."

"Well, I was just on di island," and I did some figuring of my own, "three days ago, at least I think, and no one has seen him since he left there, the day he first went to see your son."

"That is most troubling," said Rafael.

"Yes, it is," I agreed.

"You know, I don't see why he didn't at least call at some point during all this, to let someone know what the hell was going on," said Gus.

"Chester hates phones; loathes them, in fact, although I'm not sure that would have been a good enough reason for him to keep everyone worrying," I said.

"I offered to let him use my cell, but he said he didn't want to spoil the surprise of the ring," said Rafael.

"And we keep forgetting he's marginally insane," I said. "He's evidently obsessed with keeping this engagement ring shopping trip of his top secret."

"Let me go and make a call, and see if I can find out what happened after they left here," said Rafael. "Excuse me."

Rafael went into the house, and Gus and I were left alone with our Mimosas.

I took a sip of my drink and watched a blue hummingbird buzz around a bed of Mariposas, before zipping off to parts unknown. "You know, if I ever get my hands on Chester..."

"You're going to kill him?" said Gus.

"No, but I may chain him to Captain Black Dog and make him his personal guard so he can never leave di island again," I said. "It's like trying to hunt down Waldo; every time we think we've found him, he disappears into another crowd, again."

"Except Chester doesn't wear a snappy red and white striped shirt so he stands out," said Gus.

"He's gonna start, except his will be neon green and pink," I said. "And if he won't wear a real shirt, we'll hold him down and tattoo one on him."

Rafael reappeared along with one of his guards, phone in hand, and said, "This may take some time to sort out. And I'm afraid I'm going to have to ask you to leave; I've been reminded I have...associates arriving soon."

I stood up, finished my drink, gathered my beachness together, and said, "Look, Rafael, no offense; you've been a gracious host, but the two of us ain't leaving here until we know what happened to Chester."

The guard held up his gun, and Gus said, "Let me clarify. Harry meant he's not leaving; I'm outta here as soon as I can find the door."

"Thanks for having my back," I said.

"Hey, try and keep in mind that we don't like each other all that much," said Gus.

"I do already know at least that Chester did indeed leave Cuba; one of my men I just talked to saw him depart on a boat," said Rafael.

"Then where is he?" I said.

Rafael sighed. "I swear to you, I don't know," he said.

"Well, that's just wonderful," I said.

"Go home; if you give me your number, I will call the moment I know something more. But there is no point in staying in Cuba; Chester is gone from her shores," said Rafael.

"I guess I don't have any choice, do I?" I said. "Or I'm guessing you'll make me an offer I can't refuse, and I'll wake up with Starch's head next to me in my hammock."

"Starch?" said Rafael.

"Never mind," I said.

I gave Rafael my cell number, and Gus and I allowed the guard to escort us back out of the Moreno estate (although I was just about to make my move). Then we began the long walk back into town, which was luckily soon interrupted by a passing pickup full of plantation workers that picked us up, which was what pickups were supposed to do, after all.

Soon after, we checked out of the inn, my having decided to take Rafael's advice and leave Cuba while the leaving was good. Gus wanted to stay one more night, just because (Mojitos), but I insisted. While I didn't feel all that threatened by Cuba herself, I did wonder what Rafael was really capable of. And if something dastardly had happened to Chester, I could see him making a call to someone and having us arrested up and locked away to protect his son. So far, the only repressive methods we'd experienced during our stay were the Mojitos, which had definitely repressed my reflexes and several of my inhibitions, and I wanted to keep it that way.

As we soared ever higher in Gus' old Norseman and turned to the east to head towards our home ports, I was given one last good look at Cuba. I had to admit, she wasn't what I'd expected. And though I doubted I'd be heading back any time soon because of what lurked under her happy appearance, I hoped that one day things might change and I'd get the chance to return. It was such a shame that a place so lovely and vibrant, and with so much to offer, had had to suffer for so many years.

And that so many people (especially in the free U.S. of A.) were deprived of the fine rums and cigars that were now stashed in the hold of Gus' plane.

Now if only the hold would have been big enough for that nineteen fifty-six Ford Thunderbird convertible I saw for sale by the docks. In glorious Fiesta red and white.

Chapter Seventeen

"Riiiiiiiiinnnnnnnnngggggggg!!!!!!"

It would have been nice if the sound was my phone letting me know there was a call with some info about Chester, but then again that would have been heralded by Zac and Jimmy announcing they were knee deep in the water somewhere. Instead, the sound was my ears still ringing hours after standing three feet away from Captain Black Dog's little cannon when it went off, after I stupidly said I'd never seen one fired and would really like to. The Captain used the cannon to announce to di islanders there was to be a party on Jack's beach at his little tiki house in the evening, which was where we were now. About twenty of us, milling around trying to act festive, which was only working so well.

The party had been Jack's idea, something to do to raise our spirits while we waited to hear about Chester. The problem was I'd already received one phone call from Rafael, shortly before we'd landed on di island, and the news hadn't been entirely good or helpful. It seemed that he hadn't heard anything from the men who'd been tasked with bringing Chester home; in fact, he hadn't seen hide nor hair of them since. And it had been long enough now that I was beginning to wonder if Rafael would even bother finding anything more out and letting me know about it.

If he didn't, I wasn't sure how we'd find a clue as to where Chester was now or what had happened to him. I got the feeling it wouldn't be the best idea in the world to go back to Cuba or Jost or wherever we might find Luis, and try and strong arm more information from him. Rafael knew too much about where I could be found, having told most of my recent life story over breakfast at his hacienda while not talking about business.

I'd told Akiko everything I knew when we'd made landfall back on di island, and she'd taken it extremely well, all things considered. I'd left out the parts about the ring, which hadn't been easy, and it had involved a tiny amount of fibbing. I didn't think it mattered that much anyway what in particular Chester had been doing, at least for the moment; if he really never did return I'd tell her the whole story, of course. But for now, I wasn't about to be the one to spoil his surprise after all he'd done to try and keep it.

For her part, Akiko seemed to remain optimistic that Captain Crazy was alright and that he'd make it back to di island, one way or another. But for the first time in this whole mystery I wasn't so sure; it seemed like we'd come to a dead end, which while perhaps a poor choice of words, I thought described the situation pretty accurately.

All of which was keeping the party from gaining any sort of traction in the sandy beach. The grilled mahi-mahi had been tasty, as was the Captain Billy's Black Dog Rum and coke sloshing around in my mug, and Cavin and Boyd on the guitar and bongos sounded great against the backdrop of Mother Ocean's own orchestral melody. But everything was muted as if we were in a fog, with no horn or lighthouse to guide us to sunnier shores.

"This is ridiculous," said Gus, finally. "We all know Chester is fine, because Chester is always fine. He could fall into a live volcano and come out with nothing more than a nice tan."

"He already has a nice tan," said Jolly Roger.

"Then maybe his hair would grow back," said Gus. "I don't know; I just know it would somehow end up being to his advantage to get Pompeiied."

"This is different," said Jack. "Other people are involved, and they don't sound like they're a very nice bunch."

"Yeah, but Chester is," said Gus. "They'll end up liking him too much to harm a hair on his head. If he had one, that is."

"So where are you going with this, Grizwood?" I asked.

"I'm saying that we owe it to him to have a good time," said Gus.

"Don't you mean he owes it to us for us to have a good time?" I said. "Meaning you're a selfish bastard as always."

"Yeah, I mean that, too," said Gus. "And yes, I am. We've been running all over looking for Chester, facing imminent death. And I think it's about time to unwind."

"And we didn't do that in Cuba?" I said. "I don't know about you, but I was about as unwound that night as a digital watch in a hot tub."

"I have no idea what that means," said Gus.

"Neither do I," I said.

"We've done what we can. I've got to get back to hauling tourists around tomorrow, and I'm guessing you have to get back to Paradiso," said Gus.

"I'm not sure I ever *have* to get back," I said. "The Wreck doesn't exactly need me for anything to keep lazing along. But I need it, and I am looking forward to being on my beach again."

"There you go," said Gus. "So what I'm saying is, we might as well enjoy the evening and hope for the best."

"That's what I always do; hope for the best," said Jack.

"Please, none of your solar powered wisdom on how to get the most out of life," I said. "Even if you are right, most of the time. And I hate to say it, but maybe even Gus is right, just this once. I'm sure he won't make a habit of it, though."

"I tink Chester would want us to have fun, too, and not to worry," said Roger. "He'd say that every little ting is gonna be alright."

"Then since we all agree, we'll do it in his honor," said Gus, hoisting his glass high. "Here's to Chester; wherever he is, he's probably having a better time than we are, so let's party and try and keep up with him."

"Here here," said Jack.

We clinked our glasses, bottles, and mugs together, and after taking a drink, determinedly set out to have some fun.

And ten minutes later, I announced, "It just ain't happening, is it?"

"No; it's not," said not so Jolly Roger.

"I still say it was a good idea, though," said Gus.

"Did you have a back-up plan?" asked Jack.

"I always have a back-up plan," said Gus. "I'm going to just get drunk instead."

"Isn't that what you always do?" asked Roger.

"So?" said Gus. "I said I always have a back-up plan; I didn't say I had a bunch of different ones."

"More rum, den!" said Roger.

"I'll go get some," said Jack.

"Then I better go sit down if I'm gonna get serious about this," I said, and I went over and grabbed a chair around the fire pit, joined by my fellow partners in excess.

"Hey, dudes," said Moon Man, having just arrived from wherever it was he disappeared to, which was probably through some mystic portal back to Woodstock. "What's happening?"

"We've just made a group decision to get drunk," I said.

"Ah; the Chester," said Moon Man, sitting down on a chair across the fire from me. "Yeah, I heard the latest. Bummer, dude. What are you gonna do now?"

"He just told you; get drunk," said Gus. "It seems like the most useful thing at the moment."

"I tried asking the sun and the moon about Chester's whereabouts, but neither of them were very forthcoming," said Moon Man.

"Why, what did they say?" I asked, not sure I really wanted to know the answer.

"Well, it seemed like the sun was telling me to tell you to go home, Harry," said Moon Man.

"Which is what I was planning to do tomorrow, anyway," I said. "But I'm glad I have Sol's blessing to just give up."

"I'm not sure that's what he meant, but it's all I could get out of him; he stubbornly went behind a cloud and hid when I pressed him for more info," said Moon Man.

"And di moon?" asked Jolly Roger.

Moon Man sighed. "She was being all mysterious as usual; never does give a straight answer. She just said something about Chester being the key. At least that's what I think she said; Luna always whispers, and she's hard to understand. I keep telling her to speak up, but she says she doesn't want to shout like big-mouthed Sol."

"Chester's the key, huh?" I said.

"Yeah, pretty unhelpful, right? I said we already knew that, but she just kept repeating it," said Moon Man. "She's probably going through another one of her phases again."

"So why didn't you ask Mother Ocean or Ma Earth?" I said, glancing over and watching them for a moment as they flirted with one another at the shoreline.

"They both stopped speaking to me back in the seventies," said Moon Man, glumly.

"Something you said?" said Gus.

"Something we did," said Moon Man. "They're both pretty peeved at the way we've all been treating them."

"Can't say I blame them," said Jack, finally reappearing with rum reinforcements.

"Where the hell have you been?" said Gus. "Did you go all the way back to the factory and make more of the stuff or what? My fuel tank's running on E here."

"I ran into Captain Billy Black Dog," said Jack, while going over and refueling Gus' tank. "He was lurking around the rum supply in my hut and wanted to know about Chester."

"Don't we all," I said. "As much as I hate to do it, I'll keep my cell phone charged and with me for the next few days. If anyone finds anything out, we should let one another know. Agreed?"

"Agreed," agreed everyone.

"The sacrifices we make for Chester; now we're all carrying cell phones," said Jack.

"Do you think he'd put on shoes and a shirt for one of us?" I asked.

"We did see him wear flippers and a coconut bra once," said Jack.

"When was that?" I asked, really wishing I hadn't missed it.

"A couple of years ago in Key West," said Jack.

"Oh, yeah; the trip I wasn't invited on," I said.

"Hey, as I've told you a million times, I barely knew you back then!" said Jack.

"And who wants to bring a son of di beach like you along, anyway?" said Gus.

"Well, this son of di beach is gonna get down to some serious rumrunning here, meaning the rum better run for cover," I said, and I raised my glass. "To Crazy Chester, wherever he is; no shoe or shirt will ever disgrace his person, but he'll put on a bra and webbed feet for a friend."

"Who wouldn't?" said Gus.

Chapter Eighteen

"Miss Swann, for sure," said Kian.

"No way, mon; too skinny," said Keyon. "Angelica, she has all di right curves in all di right places," said Keyon.

"But you can't trust Angelica; she be stabbin' you in di back and stealin' di rum di first time she gets di chance," said Kian.

"But at least she not be burning all di rum and all di trees," argued Keyon. "With Angelica, di rum might be gone, but you can try and get it back from her, and dat be di fun part."

"Oh yeah? And do you be lookin' forward to goin' home with Angelica to meet her daddy, Captain Blackbeard?" said Kian. "Him won't be givin' you di keep your hands off my daughter speech; him just cut off your hands and be done wit it."

"Den I can get di pirate hooks; Angelica, she be likin' dat, I tink," said Keyon.

I was home again.

Gus had dropped me off back on Paradiso Shores early this morning; too damned early, if you asked me, and things were just as they should be. Kian and Keyon were in full debate mode, Maggie was reading the paper, Starch was begging for food, and the fisherman was catnapping in one of the hammocks.

The only thing missing was Crazy Chester, who wouldn't have been there in the first place.

"I gotta go with Kian on this one; he won with the meet the parents argument," I said. "And I prefer Elizabeth myself, anyway. Not that I'd be disinclined to acquiesce to any of Angelica's proposals."

"You always pick Kian!" complained Keyon.

"Dat be because I always be right," said Kian.

"No, dat be because you're ugly and he feels sorry for ya," said Keyon.

"So what's your plan for today, Harry?" asked Maggie, setting her Free Press aside. "More looking for Crazy Chester in all the wrong places?"

"Not unless there was some news about him in your paper," I said. "I'm afraid I'm out of ideas. No, I'm just going to do whatever it is I normally do around here."

"In other words, nothing," said Maggie.

"Pretty much," I said. "Any particular reason why you're interested?"

"I was thinking about going through the Keyhole for some swimming, and wondered if you wanted to join me," said Maggie.

The Keyhole was a natural, although unnatural looking, formation of caves in a cliff wall on the far side of the island, with a large, roughly skeleton keyhole shaped opening, which the ocean flowed into.

170

Paradiso Shores, like the roof of my bar, was lopsided; instead of having its higher elevation towards the center, it rose up on one end. If an ice age ever hit, we could just take down a few palm trees and we'd have a decent ski slope for beginners.

"That's tempting," I said. "But I promised to give everyone else here the afternoon off."

"Since you've been gallivanting around di Caribbean for di last few days having fun, it be only fair," said the fisherman, rousing himself from the inclined position in his net.

"Yeah, I've been a real jerk," I said. "But it is my turn to watch the store, I'll admit. Adeline must be watching yours?"

"Yes," said Maggie. "I guess I'm on my own for the day, then."

"You could come fishing with us tree, instead," said Kian. "Dat be okay with you, me brother?"

"Of course, mon," said Keyon. "Fisherman?"

"Sure ting; Maggie always be welcome," said the fisherman, his eyes lighting up. "Fishing be better den swimming, anyway. I can still manage to stay afloat with me wooden leg, but it's a pain in di ass having a bobber for a limb."

"Thanks for the invite. But we might as well take my boat if we're going to have a full crew," said Maggie.

"And if I'm gonna be abandoned by everyone, you also might as well beat it now," I said. "I could use some peace and quiet around here."

"For a nap," said Maggie, getting up.

"Damned right; I deserve one," I said.

"Have fun," she said, and the quartet slowly got themselves together and headed off towards the road. And moments later, I knew they were gone when Maggie's truck started and rumbled fully out of earshot.

Starch deserted me as well, flying off to probably flirt with that cockatiel he'd had his eyes on. I was totally alone for the first time in days, and it actually felt good. Although any aliens landing on the Earth might find it hard to believe after observing humans driving, walking, sitting in bars, and pushing shopping carts around Target stores with cell phones glued to their ears, people need to be alone now and again. It gives them time to think, which in turn makes them smarter. Which might explain why our species keeps getting dumber, given how crammed together we are these days and how irritably connected we all insist upon staying.

I wandered around my beach in my solitude for a while, adjusting a few chairs so I could at least claim to have done something useful with my day. Then I decided to take a dip in Mother Ocean, remembering when I was up to my knees in her to get back out and take the phone out of my pocket before diving fully back in.

I mucked about like flipper for a while, floating here and there in the clear, blue green waters, feeling totally refreshed upon my exit and ready for a high-powered island day. Then I did all the work necessary to open the Wreck for business, meaning I took down the boards that we hung up to keep the elements more or less out of the interior at night, cleared away the mess from the morning breakfast, poured myself a coconut rum and pineapple juice, and plopped down on a bar stool.

I could tell it was going to be another gorgeous day in the Caribbean, although you usually didn't have to have much meteorological schooling to predict that correctly. It even felt the slightest bit cooler this late morning, which, while I enjoyed the heat, was always welcome as long as it didn't get carried away and lop off enough degrees to remind me of a fall day back in BPS (Before Paradiso Shores).

I decided I'd dig out my Kindle, hit the hammock, and read one of the many mysteries I'd loaded up on on one of my trips to di island, where there were now actually spots you could hook up to the internet (okay, I'd had to get a room at the Wind Song Resort to do so, but it had been worth it to get some new reading material). I preferred a real book in my hands, but since there wasn't exactly a nearby store to keep running off to every time I had the urge to read something new, it was a good enough alternative. It was strange though how an electronic device actually helped me live this castaway lifestyle I enjoyed; without it, I'd be stuck reading the same books over and over. But this way, I had a small library in my hands, and I think Robinson Crusoe would have seriously considered trading Friday for a loaded Kindle or Nook if he could have. As long as the natives had had one of the new solar powered ones for barter, that is.

I made the huge effort necessary to turn on the mp3 player and the boombox it was plugged into behind the bar, another pair of my little technological island helpers, and got some trop rock and reggae sounds going. Then I sat and played bar patron slash tender, drank my drink, told myself a couple of bawdy jokes, paid my tab, tipped myself, and washed and put away my glass. Then I headed towards the Anchored Away to get my library.

As I walked by one of the picnic tables, my phone happened to beep at me from where it lay upon it. I considered ignoring it, but knew it would just keep it up if I didn't at least pat it on the head for letting me know I'd had some sort of a message in a digital bottle from the outside world. So I went over and picked it up, and after checking it, found I'd missed a call from Jack. Several, in fact, which, judging by the time, must have come while I was playing porpoise in the sea.

He'd left me a voice mail as well, but I hated listening to those; if I was going to talk on the damned thing, I at least wanted it to be to a live person. So instead I called him back, and a few rings later we were talking island to island, and without two tin cans and a really long string.

"Harry! I've been trying to get a hold of you," said Jack.

"No kidding; you don't suppose that's why I'm talking to you now, do ya?" I said. "What's so bloody important? And please don't tell me you've had another epiphany about rum and its relationship to a healthy soul, because I already know about it."

"You're not going to believe this, but I got a call an hour or so ago about Crazy Chester," said Jack. "From a guy demanding ransom money."

"That's good news!" I said.

"It is? How do you figure?" said Jack.

"Well, it's better than him being missing, isn't it?" I said. "Technically, he's not lost anymore. At least, not *as* lost."

"I guess that's one way of looking at it," said Jack.

"Hey, you're the one with the positive attitude, so I shouldn't have to tell you these things; I'm the son of di beach, remember? Try and keep up." I said. "So what did they say?"

"They said they're holding Chester, and that they'll call back and tell me where and when they want me to deliver the money," said Jack.

"Did they say what they'd do if you didn't comply?" I said.

"No; I suppose not. I just assumed the worst, I guess. Why would they do anything but kill him?" said Jack.

"I don't know; it would just be refreshing if the kidnappers threatened something else for a change, like they'd take him out for a really lousy dinner if they didn't get the cash," I said. "Or to listen to karaoke."

"This is serious!" said Jack. "Stop making jokes."

"I know," I said. "I wonder why they called you, and not Akiko, though?"

"Probably because I own the rum factory and the sugar plantation; everyone thinks I'm rich, for some reason," said Jack.

"You kind of are, at least compared to everyone else around here," I said. "So are you going to pay them?"

"Yeah, I am. I don't really have much choice, do I?" said Jack. "And anyway, I'm glad to, to get Chester back."

"Do you have enough? You're not calling me for money, are you? Because I'm not really swimming in cash. I'll help if I can, but I have to keep any nibbling at my nest egg to a minimum, since it's gotta last," I said. "What did they ask for, anyway?"

"That's the weird thing," said Jack. "It wasn't really that big an amount."

"So how much, then?" I said.

"Four thousand, three hundred and seventy-two dollars. And forty-two cents," said Jack.

"That's it?" I said.

"Yep," said Jack.

"Amateurs," I said, comparing the situation to every mystery I'd ever read. "Why would anybody kidnap someone for that piddly amount?"

"I don't know. But that's why I'm not balking too much about paying it," said Jack. "I'm just going to wait until they call back, and do whatever they say. I am anxious to talk to Chester, though, if it all works out, and find out who the heck it was."

Something was running around in the back of my mind, some memory of a number trying to attach itself to something in my noggin'. I let it dig around in my hold for a while, then suddenly it started to wave its arms around frantically as a tiki torch lit up in my head.

"I don't think you have to wait to find out who it is," I said.

"Really?" said Jack. "Why's that?"

"Because I *know* who it is," I said.

"You know who's got Chester?" said Jack. "How can you possibly know that?"

"Because I do," I said. "And not only that, but I've got a pretty good idea where he is."

"And where might that be?" said Jack.

"About a mile from where I'm standing," I said. "Just stay where you are, and in the meantime, agree to whatever they say. I'll handle this."

Chapter Nineteen

Maggie and I squatted in the bushes together, something I didn't normally do with another person. Although if I was gonna do so with anybody, Mags would have been my first choice. But while bathrooms were pretty spread out on Paradiso Shores, there was more than enough shrubbery that you wouldn't have to share a leafy stall if you had a sudden emergency.

Of course, that's not why we were squatting in the nighttime jungle at the moment; we were squatting because for some reason that's what you did when you were hiding in bushes. We were currently on a recon mission, on the south side of the enemy's compound, while Kian snooped around to the west and Keyon checked things out to the north.

Maggie had insisted on coming along, and I'd insisted in return that she stay by my side. The fisherman had wanted to come and help too, but someone needed to watch the Wreck, or at least that's what I told him. The truth was that I closed the place whenever I felt like it and it never seemed to bring the world crashing to an end. But the fisherman wasn't known for his ability to keep quiet, since he was hard of hearing to go along with his single eye vision and one legged mobility, and I knew the tiniest degree of stealth was in order.

It was pretty obvious that our self-proclaimed island governor and fearless leader Cosimo Berardi was the villain who'd shanghaied Chester, or was the most recent one who had, anyway. The ransom was identical to the amount Maggie had said he was looking to raise for his newest tourist PR fiasco.I was surprised Cosimo had gone that far, however; most of the crimes he'd committed in the past had been in his head, meaning I'd thought he was simply a mostly harmless nutjob who perhaps should've been committed himself. He and his mob didn't really scare much of anyone, and we'd let him swagger about because aside from a stolen, or more precisely borrowed without permission and then re-retrieved bicycle or two, it had been nothing but words. But now suddenly he'd crossed the line into something approaching real crime.

I didn't know for sure how Paradiso's poor man's Italian Don had come to nab Chester in the first place, but I had my suspicions. I figured it had actually been two of Cosimo's men who Luis, back in Cuba, had ended up hiring to take Chester home to di island. And that Cosimo had simply rerouted him here to Paradiso Shores, using the same sort of technique the airlines did with your luggage.

That part was a little bit disturbing. First, that one of Cosimo's men would be all the way over in

Cuba doing who knows what, second, that he evidently had more men than I'd previously realized, and third, that he would somehow know the Moreno family. It seemed like it meant that Governor Berardi was tinkering with becoming a real live criminal. Which was why I was being cautious now and hunkering down in the foliage, instead of simply walking down the road, banging on the door, and demanding Chester's freedom from the pompous, roly-poly little shit.

"What do you think?" asked Maggie.

"I think I hate bugs," I said, swatting yet another one as it nibbled on my thigh. "And that flip-flops are gonna be lousy protection if a viper comes along and decides to suck on one of my toes."

"I tried to tell you that, but you wouldn't listen, as usual," said Maggie. "That's why I'm wearing my work boots."

"My feet spent too many years incarcerated in wing-tips; they'd go mental on me if I tried to lock them back up now," I said.

"Your choice. But I do agree with you about the insects," said Maggie, doing some swatting of her own. "Anyway, I haven't seen a single person go in or out of the building. Or anyone moving around inside, for that matter. Have you?"

"No, but that doesn't mean there aren't ten men in there with sub-machine guns purchased from the Moreno family," I said.

"Yeah, but you'd think we'd have seen at least one of them head to the outhouse by now," said Maggie.

"We've only been here a couple of hours," I said. "And I'm not going to try and estimate their manpower based solely on trips to the loo."

"I don't know how else we're gonna find out," said Mags. "Unless we sneak up and look in the window."

"Yeah, like that'll work," I said, looking at the small, stilted house in the clearing. "Damn it! I just want to know how many evil knights are in there before we storm the castle."

"None," said a voice, scaring me half to death.

I whirled around, something I rarely get to do, and found half a set of twins on my port side.

"Keyon!" I hissed. "Don't sneak up on me like that. And how do you know there's no one inside?"

"I went up and looked in di window," said Keyon.

"See?" said Maggie.

"How'd you manage that? We've been watching the building the whole time and we didn't even see you," I said.

"Which just goes to show how useful this is," said Maggie.

"Hey, you wanted to come along," I said.

"Actually, I wanted you to not come here at all, but like I said, you never listen to me," said Maggie.

"I just snuck up on di porch and peeked inside; very dark," said Keyon.

"What about Chester; did you see him in there?" I asked, knowing that if I didn't question him about it, chances were he wouldn't tell me.

"He just said it was dark, dumb-dumb," said Maggie.

"No, mon, I didn't see anyone at all, but he could be in di back room, di one on di north corner with di windows boarded shut so you can't see inside," said Keyon.

"And there could be a bunch of men in there, as well," I said.

Keyon shrugged. "Anyting is possible," he said.

"Any sign of Cosimo?" asked Mags.

"No, but he could be in di other back room with di shades pulled down," said Keyon.

"Which is another spot that could hide more men," I said. "How the hell do they make this work in the movies? Stake out a place, I mean?"

"For starters, I don't think they bother with someone like Cosimo," said Maggie. "I don't know why you're being so paranoid about him all of a sudden. He's about as dangerous as an overstuffed cannelloni. Or is it his toucan again?"

"Hey, that bird is the devil's spawn," I said. "I can see it in his beady little eyes."

"If you feel that way about it, why don't we all just chip in and pay the ransom and be done with it?" said Maggie. "It's not that much, really, and if Cosimo is going to put it towards promoting Paradiso, what's the big deal? Or don't pay him at all; I'm sure he'd never hurt Chester, anyway. But just let him play his gangster games."

"I refuse," I said. "It's a matter of principal, like the guy who kept robbing my stores back in the states. I finally just had to stop him."

"And did dat turn out to be a good idea?" said Keyon.

I reached down and rubbed my leg, verifying I could still feel the scar from that particular escapade. "That depends on how you look at it. He didn't rob any more of my shops after that, and I survived. Hurt like hell though, and I was lucky it didn't turn out worse. But if we give in to Cosimo, who knows what he'll try next. No, we gotta make a stand and draw a line in the sand, and say this stops here and now!"

"Very inspiring; it was just like listening to Churchill," said Maggie, dryly. She smited another bug, and asked, "So are we going in or not?"

"Not," I said. "Yet, anyway."

"Then I'm outta here," said Mags. "If we're not going to do anything, I don't see the point; you can stay out here all night and get eaten if you want. Are you coming, Keyon?"

"Yeah, but let me go get me brother, first," said Keyon.

"Stop by my place and I'll have something cool waiting for you guys," said Maggie. "Have fun playing bug buffet, Harry. We'll see you at the Wreck for breakfast tomorrow."

"Thanks a lot," I said, and I watched the two disappear into the shrubbery in their respective directions.

I couldn't blame them for leaving, though, and truth be known, it was what I'd wanted them to do. It was obvious we weren't going to figure out who was in Cosimo's house, anytime soon, anyway. Which meant we'd have to go inside without knowing and hope there wouldn't be seventeen gunmen playing poker squeezed into the back room, and I didn't want to put Mags or the K twins at risk. This way it would only be me, which would be enough if it was just Cosimo. And if it wasn't just him, well, then the others wouldn't have mattered anyway.

I waited about fifteen minutes to make sure my friends had vacated the area, then crept slowly towards the building. It was quiet; too quiet, especially with flip-flops. Sneaking while wearing them would have been a lot easier through, say, a construction site or missile range, than this dead silent clearing where I could hear every rubbery step. The stairs made annoying creaks as I climbed up them, too, sounding to my ears like a rusty chainsaw. As did the rickety porch, and I was sure the three steps it took me to cross it had heralded my presence to everyone within a five mile radius. But eventually I stood stock still before the front door, listening for any noises to come from the inside.

None did, and I was satisfied that at least no one had heard me. That didn't mean there still couldn't be a crowd of thugs in there; they could all be quietly playing bridge instead of a rowdy game of poker. Or they could have been reading the collective works of Emily Dickinson or Robert Frost. You didn't want to go around stereotyping goons; it pissed them off to no end. But I did feel a little safer now that I could hear that there was nothing I could hear.

I took my Swiss Army knife out of my pocket and chose a normal blade to try and pop the door open.

I jiggled and pried for a few moments then thought to try the doorknob, which wasn't locked, yet another good reason not to have Mags along since she would have never let me hear the end of it. I turned the knob ever so slowly, then swung the door open quickly to avoid any prolonged creaking.

It was the first moment of truth, but all I saw was a dark room. If there were any hooligans in the shadows, they seemed more intent on suddenly turning on the lights, yelling, *"Surprise!"*, and singing happy birthday before shooting me. As it was I was fairly sure I was simply alone.

I tiptoed across the floor through the furniture, not easy to do in my flips, over to the door that led to the back north corner room Keyon had mentioned. I slowly opened it, and found it did indeed lead to a bedroom of sorts, with a cot in one corner. From what I could barely see in the darkness, it looked like there was a figure under the blankets, and I crept over to the side of the bed.

The door I'd entered through suddenly closed with a fairly loud click, which just about made me jump through the ceiling. When my heart finally stopped racing I knelt down in the dim light and placed my hands on the blanket to shake it. It didn't feel right, meaning it didn't feel at all Chester-ish or any other person-ish. I pulled the blanket back and found a pile of clothes underneath, and realized I was trying to wake someone's dirty laundry, probably Cosimo's. That hadn't been what I'd had in mind on several levels, and I stood up and wiped my hands on my shorts, as if that would help. I looked around the room, and after hazarding a hissed "Chester!" decided that he wasn't in there, and headed back towards the door to get out while the getting was good.

The getting didn't turn out to be so good after all, however, since the door was now thoroughly locked. I swore under my breathe, pushed and pulled on the knob, but to no avail. I was about to call on the Swiss Army to come to my rescue again, when I saw light suddenly come streaming across the wooden floor from the main room from beneath the door. And seconds later, the small speakeasy style sliding window in the door that I hadn't seen in the dark slid open, and I heard Cosimo's gruff Italian voice say, "Who da hell's in dere?"

Chapter Twenty

I tried to come up with something clever to say, hoping at the very least to not seem like the total idiot that I'd suddenly become, but nothing sprang to mind. Instead, I simply said, "It's me."

"Me? Who da hell is me? Or is dat you, Captain Harry?" said Cosimo.

"Yeah, it's Harry," I said. "You want to let me out of here?"

"You wanna tell me what you're doin' in dere, first?" said Cosimo.

"Alright; I guess I don't have much choice," I said. "I was looking for Crazy Chester."

Cosimo was silent on his side of the door for a moment, then he burst out laughing. "Ha, ha! You came to rescue him, and instead you got locked in my back room, didn't ya?" he said. "What a goombah!"

"No argument there," I said. "What is this place, anyway? Why does it close and lock from the outside? And why the high security, like the metal plate around the lock, and the little *"What's the secret password?"* door?"

"It's da room I keep Corleone in," I said.

"Corleone!" I said, frantically looking around in the dim light. "You mean that crazy ass toucan is in here with me?"

189

"Relax; I only put him in dere when I'm gonna be gone for some time and can't take him wit me," said Cosimo. "Otherwise, he's out here."

"Well, I could see why you might want the door to close automatically then, but why the lock on the inside? He can't open doors too, can he?" I said.

"No, but I wanna catch anyone who tries to steal him," said Cosimo.

"Who'd want that scraggly, big-nosed piece of poultry?" I said.

"Careful, Harry; remember, you're on da inside, and I'm on da outside. If you want out, you're gonna hav'ta play nice," said Cosimo.

"Sorry," I said, reluctantly. "So you are going to let me out, then?"

There was a pause, then Cosimo finally said, "No. Not right now, anyway."

I grabbed the door knob and pulled and pushed as hard as I could, but it barely budged, and I could tell I'd have about as much luck trying to get it open as I had Cynthia Clarke's bra back in ninth grade. "Let me out of here, you little twerp!" I yelled, resorting to pounding on the door. I finally gave that up, too, and turned around and leaned my back on it instead and slid to the floor to sit.

"Are ya finished throwin' your fit?" said Cosimo.

"Yeah, I'm good for now," I said. "Can you tell me something, though?"

"Maybe; if you ask nice," said Cosimo, who was obviously enjoying this.

"Where is Chester?" I said.

It was silent for a moment, then Cosimo said, "I have no idea."

"No idea? It was you who called Jack and demanded a ransom for him, wasn't it?" I said.

"Me? I don't know what you're talking about," said Cosimo.

"Come on; come clean. You've got me locked in here in an impossible to escape situation; now it's time for you, the bad guy, to reveal your evil plot," I said. "So admit it; you did call Jack, didn't you?"

"Yes, I did. But I didn't ask for a ransom," said Cosimo.

"Then what did you do?" I asked.

"I called and said, *"Is Crazy Chester missing?"* Then I waited for dat to sink in, and said, *"I need four thousand, three hundred and seventy-two dollars,"*" said Cosimo

"And forty-two cents," I said.

"Exactly," said Cosimo. "Jack must'a thought I had Chester, for some reason."

"Yeah, for *some* reason," I said. "So you never said the money was for a ransom?"

"Nope," said Cosimo. "He just assumed. And you know what happens when you assume."

"Not that I approve, but that's almost clever. Not the part where you just called yourself an ass, but the phone call," I said. "But the question remains; where the hell is Chester?"

"I don't know. I just heard he was missing, and thought dat Jack might want to donate some money for da new billboards," said Cosimo. "And now dat I have you, he might want to help pay for some newspaper ads, too."

I stood back up, and addressed Cosimo face to hole to face again. "No, you're going to let me out of here, and now, or there's going to be hell to pay!" I said.

"Really? You're da one who broke into my house uninvited," said Cosimo. "As governor, I should have ya incarcerated."

"You're not the governor! Get that through your thick skull once and for all!" I shouted. "And should I have broken into your house invited?"

"Well, it's late, and I'm tired of talkin' wit you, and I need to get some sleep; got a big day tomorrow. You can use da bed if you want, and if you need it, dere's a bucket in da corner," said Cosimo. "Buona Notte." And he abruptly slid the peep hole shut, and soon after, the light went off in the living room.

I spent the next hour or so rotating through banging on the wall to try and keep Cosimo from sleeping, using every gadget and gizmo the Swiss had to offer on the door, and yelling for help through one of the cracks between the boards on the window. None of which seemed particularly useful, except for perhaps the banging on the wall, since payback was the one thing I could get started on now.

I did manage to find a light switch, but the hole of a room I was in was so depressing that I turned it back off; I could see now why Corleone was so cantankerous. But it made me calm down enough to think straight, and I realized that it would only be a matter of time before somebody came looking for me. Mags and the twins knew where I was, and eventually they should figure out that something must have gone wrong. At least Mags would; Kian and Keyon might decide I'd gone fishing somewhere, which was what most people on Paradiso assumed you were off doing if they couldn't find you. Then again, Maggie might decide to teach me a lesson, and just leave me in Cosimo's clutches for a while. I wasn't sure what lesson that would be, but I was sure she could come up with something.

Either way, there was nothing I could do about it for now. Spending the entire night banging, yelling, scratching, and prying wasn't going to get me anything but tired in the morning. So I gingerly removed all of Cosimo's garments from the cot, took off my hat, and laid down to try and get some shuteye.

I fell asleep surprisingly quickly, all things considered; I guess all my crouching and skulking and clattering around had tuckered me out. But I dreamt me some tumultuous dreams of dark figures, spine tingling sensations, and shadows that only slunk away to hide from the daylight that came streaming through the boards on the windows, when my eyes finally reopened many hours later. Or maybe it wasn't the daylight they slunk away from, but the presence of the shirtless, shoeless man who stood over my cot. Making me wonder if he would never wear a shirt, if he could at least be talked into wearing a cape. Or maybe allow a big red "S" to be tattooed on his chest.

"Well, are you gonna lay there sleeping all day, or do ya want to be rescued?" said Crazy Chester, my superhero.

Chapter Twenty-One

I sat up in my cot, and looked around and noticed that my accommodations were even dingier than I'd thought. And that Chester had been smart enough to prop the door open. "Where the hell have you been?" I said, which while perhaps not the standard greeting for batmen, firemen, police men, or any other rescue type men, seemed a valid enough question.

"That's a long story," said Chester.

"Yeah, it is, and I've been reading it over the last few days," I said, as I climbed out of bed. "I'm dying to see how it ends."

"Then let's get out of here and go find out," said Chester.

"Sounds good to me," I said, grabbing my Panama hat and sticking it on my head before sliding my feet into my flip-flops. "After I kick the Ricotta out of Cosimo, that is."

"He's not here," said Chester. "I'll explain once we're clear of this place; come on."

We made our way outside and down the path from Cosimo's property to the road. It felt good to be free again and back amongst the palm trees instead of Cosimo's grubby undies. "So what's going on? How did you find me? And where the hell is my Italian jailer?" I asked, as we walked along.

"Cosimo called Jack this morning and told him to bring the money and lower it into the Pit," said Chester. "At least I think that's what the place is called."

"If you mean the well the idiot had his men, or man, start to dig, then yeah," I said. "I told him he was too close to the beach and that he'd only run into sea water, and for once he listened to me and stopped. But not before he'd dug a ten foot hole in the ground."

"That's the one, I guess. Jack knew what he was talking about, anyway. The thing is, though, I'd already gotten back to di island by the time Cosimo called," said Chester. "Arrived early this morning."

"I'm dying to know from where, but let's finish all the stuff from around here, first," I said. "Like how you knew where I was."

"Jack tried to call you to let you know what was going on with the ransom, but Maggie answered. She had your phone, I guess?" said Chester.

"Uh, yeah, I realized that last night while I was in lockdown. I gave it to her to use as a flashlight while we traipsed through the jungle, and I guess she stuck it in her pocket," I said. "For once, I could have actually used the damn thing."

"That's what Maggie said, that she had it by mistake," said Chester. "And she told Jack where she'd left you, and that knowing you, you'd managed to get into some sort of trouble, since you were awol this morning."

"That's my girl," I said. "Always brimming with confidence in my ability to screw things up."

"The rest is pretty simple. I just rode along when Jack and the others came to Paradiso to deliver the money, and snuck off over to Cosimo's place and found you there," said Chester.

"Jack came here to bring the money anyway?" I said. "Is he nuts? Cosimo doesn't need this to turn out good for him."

"Don't worry," said Chester. "Everything's well in hand, so to speak."

I finally looked around, and noticed that we hadn't been heading towards my place, but in the opposite direction. "What are we doing here?" I said. "Wait a minute; this is near the Pit, isn't it?"

"Yep," said Chester, with a smile. "I thought you might want to see."

"See? See what?" I said.

"Go and see, see?" said Chester, pointing at the little path that went into the bushes. "I'll be waiting here where it's safe."

"Safe from what?" I said.

"You'll find out," said Chester. "You can't miss it, believe you me."

"Okay; anything you say," I said.

I pushed my way through the bushes that lined the trail, and did soon find out as I suddenly had to pinch my nose shut against a rancid stench that seemed to be coming from all around me, "That's just nasty," I said aloud and to myself, as I emerged at the clearing near the well. "But where's it coming from?"

"The Pit, Captain Harry; where else?" said a pirate.

"Captain Black Dog!" I exclaimed in a rather nasally voice, as he stepped from behind a tree. "What are you doing here?"

"Guarding the prisoner," said Black Dog.

"You don't mean that...you didn't...did you?" I said.

Captain Billy Black Dog pointed at the hole in the ground. "Aye, we did. Me and me crew, that is. Jumped out and waylaid the blaggard about an hour ago. One of the best times of me life, finally gettin' to waylay somebody. See for yerself."

I walked tentatively forward, afraid the pungent odor might snatch me and pull me down into the depths, and peered over the edge.

"I'll give ya anything ya want. Corleone, da governorship, control of my mob; anything! If ya just get me outta here," Cosimo said up to me, from the bottom of the Pit.

"I can't say that I blame you," I said, now face to face with the stench. "But the tables are turned now, and it serves you right. So where's your duck of death?"

"He took off before we even got near dis place," said Cosimo. "I should have read dat as an early warning sign and flown away myself."

"I suppose with that nose of his he realized those weren't Fruit Loops wafting on the breeze," I said. "But what is that smell, anyway?"

"Yesterday's lunch special at Robichaux's," said Black Dog. "Some kind of fish and stinky, runny cheese, pasta combo. I heard it was really tasty, but the smell put people off so bad there was quite a bit left over. It was sittin' out back of his place, and Henri gladly donated it for the cause."

"And I suppose it's gotten worse yet hanging in that bag in the heat," I said, pointing at the burlap sack that hung a foot or so above Cosimo's head.

"Aye, I can testify to that," said Black Dog. "I've been tryin' to stay downwind of it, but it doesn't exactly need a typhoon to carry it. It's like a ghost ship of stink, and it could take down the Kraken."

"Where did the rest of the pirates go," I asked.

"If ya mean Jack and the lot, they all went back to di island; something about having real lives," said Black Dog. "Although I'm guessin' it had more to do with the stench than anything."

I glanced down into the pit of despair again at Cosimo. He looked miserable down there in his three piece, creamsicle colored suit with matching shoes and fedora hat. I actually felt sorry for him, and I walked carefully around the edge of the hole to Billy Black Dog's side to speak privately to him.

"I was just wondering; how long are you planning to keep him down there?" I asked.

"We figured that's up to you, mate," said Black Dog. "Seein' as how you're the most aggrieved party, here."

"You know, being me, normally I'd say to leave him for a week. But now that I've seen him," and I took a whiff, "and smelled his surroundings, the words cruel and unusual punishment come to mind. I don't want to end up doling out Castro like abuse."

"So do you want me to throw him a rope and get him out of there?" said Black Dog.

I thought about it. "No, not yet; he did make me sleep with his underwear, and that had a rather lively fragrance of its own. Go ahead and let him experience our own repressive methods for a while, say, til around nightfall. Just make sure he has something to eat and drink."

"He's already got water, and I never planned to let him starve, although I'm not sure he'll have much of an appetite," said Black Dog. "Especially for pasta," he added, with a toothy grin.

"Thanks, Captain," I said. "If you need anything, Maggie should be just down the beach at Hockeytown."

"Aye; talked to the bonnie lass an hour or so ago," said Black Dog. "Right before she said she needed to go take a shower or three."

"Then since you've got things well in hand here, I'm off," I said.

"Fair winds to ye, Captain Harry," said Black Dog.

"They're bound to be fairer than these," I said. Then I saluted him, gave Cosimo a little *"ta-ta"* wave followed by an Italian bras d'honneur fist pump, and happily made my back to where Crazy Chester stood patiently waiting.

"So; do you approve?" said Chester.

"I'd have to say yes, though I almost feel guilty about it, for some reason," I said. "Probably because even I'd have to agree with Maggie that I'm the one who got myself into this mess in the first place. Of course, Cosimo could have just let me out, too."

"And he still needed to be punished for trying to scam Jack out of the money," said Chester. "If you want, we'll say that that's why he's stuck in that pothole of putridness."

"Works for me; I'm sure not gonna lose any sleep over it," I said. "No more than I have already, anyway." Then I put my hand on Chester's shoulder, both as a sign of affection, and to make sure he wasn't about to go running off somewhere again.

"Then what now?" said Chester.

"Now, my traveling, adventuring, disappearing friend, let's get over to the Wreck," I said, then I gave myself a smell, and added, "I need a bath of my own; those were some odorific hours I just spent. And I'm feeling famished. But most of all, Lucy, you've got a helluva lot of 'splainen' to do!"

Chapter Twenty-Two

A cold shower behind the Rumwreck followed by a quick dip in Mother Ocean later, and I was feeling refreshed and relatively odor free, expect for the lovely salt water smell. Then I hit the grill and seared up some jerk chicken for Chester, the fisherman and I, and finally sat down at a table in the sand to eat and relax.

We ate in silence for a few moments, savoring the spicy sweet taste, until I could no longer contain my questions. Finally I said, "Alright, Chester; it's time to spill the beans."

Chester looked down quizzically at his plate, where his red beans lay next to his half eaten jerk sandwich.

"Not those; I want you to spill the beans that you've been carrying with you all over the Caribbean," I said.

"Where do you want me to start?" said Chester.

"How about at the beginning, back on the morning you disappeared, so I can put it all in retrospect," I said.

"Ya, mon; bring it on," said the fisherman.

"Alright; I got out of bed that day like normal, about four AM," said Chester.

"No, not normal, especially for an islander, but we'll let that pass for now," I said.

"I got cleaned up, puttered around the house for a bit, then went down to open my bar. But I found out we didn't have enough Bloody Mary mix, so I headed towards the docks at Robichaux's to grab Boyd's boat and putt out to Jack's place to get some," said Chester.

"Why didn't you just borrow it from the Innkeeper next door?" I said.

Chester looked at me as if I'd just suggested he strip naked, dip himself in motor oil, and sing "*Pink Cadillac*" while massaging an iguana.

"Dey don't get along so well, do dey, dumb dumb?" said the fisherman.

"No," I said. "I guess they don't. But don't call me dumb."

"Den don't *be* dumb," said the fisherman.

"I walked down the beach to the docks, then sailed out to di Isla De Luis," said Chester.

"And on the way, stopped and made sure a touron under a bush wasn't dead," I said.

Chester thought about it. "Oh yeah; forgot about about Dave," he said.

"You remember his name?" I said.

"I remember everyone's name, especially my customers; don't you?" said Chester.

"I'm not even gonna comment on that," I said. "When all I do is try and forget all the idiots who show up at my place."

"Come, on; you don't fool anybody. We all know you like to have di people come to di bar," said the fisherman. "You just like pretending you're a son of di beach, but we all see your smile gets bigger when someone finally shows up."

"Only the ladies," I said.

"Uh-huh; anyting you say," said the fisherman.

"So you went out to di Isla De Luis," I said, trying to get the story moving again, since it had stalled in a sand dune.

"Yes. I went inside the bar to get the mix, and found Leo and Tion sleeping on the mats on the floor," said Chester.

"You do remember everyone's name, don't you?" I said.

"I try," said Chester. "It's something my dad taught me. Anyway, I tried to be quiet, but they woke up, and we got to talking, and they said they had to get back to Jost Van Dyke because Tion had to work. But I could tell they were still pretty rummified, and I didn't want anything to happen to them, so I offered to drive Tion's boat back for them. I still had plenty of time to get over there, catch Jolly Roger's ferry back, and help with the lunch rush."

"I knew you were too smart to fly with Gus," I said.

"I don't know about that, but on the way to Jost, I decided I would buy Akiko a ring while I was there," said Chester.

"Was that before or after you fell off the boat?" I said.

"After," said Chester, matter of factly, as if falling into the water was nothing out of the ordinary. Which for him, wasn't. "And Tion said he knew a guy who had really great deals on nice jewelry."

"Yeah, time out there," I said. "Now what made you think it'd be a good idea to go see a guy named *"the Fox"* who sells out of the back of a liquor store to buy a ring for your dearly beloved?"

Chester shrugged. "Why not?" he said.

"Oh, I don't know," I said. "Because chances are, he's a thief and a con man? Not to mention, a really bad dresser?"

"You don't know that," said Chester.

"Yes, I do; I saw him, and that shirt and pants combo he was wearing didn't go at all well together," I said.

"I meant, you don't know if he's a thief; he could be on the up and up," said Chester. "The problem with you, Harry, is you never give anyone the benefit of the doubt."

"Human nature," I said.

"Yours, or theirs?" said Chester.

"Both," I said. "My point is, an engagement ring is a pretty big deal. Even I would know not to skimp on it, and I'm against the whole idea to begin with."

"An engagement ring?" exclaimed Chester. "Who said anything about an engagement ring?"

"You weren't gonna propose to Akiko?" said the fisherman. "What are ya, an idiot? She be di perfect woman; pretty, nice, and she can bake like di wind."

"Akiko's not sure she wants to get married, though we do keep talking about it," said Chester. "But I'm not gonna push it."

"Smart girl. Although maybe she just isn't ready for a no shoes, no shirt wedding ceremony," I said. "So if it wasn't for your engagement, you were searching for a ring for her because..."

"...because it's her birthday next week," said Chester.

"Ah," I said. "I guess that makes sense, too."

"The Fox had a really nice one, with four tiny diamonds and one bigger one, but the large one was badly flawed," said Chester. "But that was alright, since I'd wanted to find a ring with an emerald anyway, and I figured I'd just replace it. And the Fox knew someone who sold stones, and he was nice enough to get a hold of him for me."

"Yeah, the Fox was a real gem himself," I said. "You know, I knew most of this, so let me try and speed this up. The guy he directed you to, his name was Luis, right?"

"Yeah. See? You do remember people's names," said Chester.

"This one was kind of hard to forget, since his name was the whole reason everything got screwy from that point on," I said. "This Luis, he forced you to go to Cuba, didn't he?"

"Forced me? No. I went because his dying grandfather, Alejandro, wanted to know about his brother, and Luis thought our Luis from di island might be him. It was the least I could do, I thought," said Chester.

"So just like that, you went; didn't call, didn't write, didn't think. You just got on a boat with a gangster and went to Cuba," I said.

"Yes," said Chester. "He said his grandpapa could go any time, so I knew we had to hurry."

"I don't think he meant that minute; you could've stopped to call and tell us where you were," I said.

"I didn't want to spoil the surprise of the ring," said Chester. "And I didn't think it would take very long."

"You were going to Cuba!" I exclaimed. "If things had gone wrong, you could've been there a very long time. Like, forever."

"Naw; it's a nice place, full of nice people," said Chester. "Like the Moreno family."

"They're gangsters," I said.

"No, they're not," said Chester. "Don't be silly."

"Yes, they are," I said. "And don't be naive; Rafael told me himself."

"You were there?" said Chester.

"Yes, I was. Jack didn't mention the fact that we'd been following your trail all over hell and gone?" I said.

Chester looked around him, and I did the same to see what he was looking at. Which turned out to be sunshine and palm trees.

"Alright; we were following your trail all over paradise and gone, then," I said. "But it doesn't have the same ring to it. Happy now?"

"Always," said Chester.

"And now we're getting to the part of the story that I don't know," I said. "Rafael said that he'd told his son, Luis, to have someone take you back to di island. But you should have been back even before I found out you were missing, so what went wrong?"

"Nothing went wrong. It just took me a while to get home," said Chester. "For starters, Alejandro, Luis, and Rafael insisted I stay and enjoy their hospitality for a couple of days, so I would have time to recall and pass on every little thing about *our* Luis. And it gave them time to get the emerald, which they ended up giving me, by the way. They even brought it to a jeweler and had it put in the ring while I was at their home."

"Okay, so the Morenos did treat you very well. And now you have ties to the Cuban mob, so if the Innkeeper gets out of line again, you can just have him whacked," I said. "And that explains two more days of being gone. But what else happened? Unless you fell off the boat every two feet, it shouldn't have taken," and I tried to figure it out, but gave up, "that many days to get back."

"No, but the defection took a while," said Chester.

"The defection," I said. "I'm just gonna sit back and let you explain that small part."

"The two men who were taking me home, Felix and Lazaro, said they were unhappy living in Cuba," said Chester. "They didn't like their jobs, for one thing."

"You mean, a career as a mobster hadn't turned out to be as rewarding as they'd always dreamed?" I said.

"I guess not," said Chester. "I told them all about the things I'd done to change my life, quitting my job managing at Walmart, buying the bar in the Keys, and then finally moving to di island. They said they wished they could do something like that, so I decided to help them."

"You know, the nickname Crazy Chester is really quite an understatement," I said. "Deranged, demented, or mad as a hatter come to mind as more accurate descriptions."

"Can I finish?" said Chester.

"If there is an end to this, then yeah, go for it," I said.

"I told them to take us to my old bar in the Keys, which is now called *"Crazy Gary's Bar and Boat Stop"*," said Chester.

"I bet Gary doesn't run around helping Cuban defectors," I said.

"He did this time," said Chester. "I introduced Felix and Lazaro to him, and he agreed to take them down to the immigration office in Key West. He didn't think it would be a good idea if I did it, since I was the one who'd brought them into America."

"Smart thinking, from at least one person involved in the fiasco," I said.

"And I stuck around to watch his bar for the day while he took care of that, since I knew the place so well," said Chester. "And it was fun being back in my old home. Then I had to return the Moreno family's boat to Cuba, since it belonged to them."

"By all means; you wouldn't want to steal from a thief," I said.

"And it took me a couple of days to find a ride back out of Cuba," said Chester.

"How you managed to un-maroon yourself from a communist country, I don't know," I said.

"And I had to find a way to get from Puerto Rico, where I ended up, over to Jost," said Chester.

"Any more ands?" I said.

"And finally, Tion gave me a ride back to di island this morning," said Chester.

"And all this without shoes or a shirt," I said.

Chester shrugged. "Who needs 'em?" he said.

"Dat all makes sense, now," said the fisherman.

"Does it?" I said. "I'm glad someone thinks so. Because I bet there's not one missionary in Africa who's had as convoluted an adventure trying to do good deeds as Round the Bend Chester just did."

"Round di Bend?" said the fisherman.

"Just trying it on for size," I said.

I gave Starch, who had been snoozing on my shoulder the whole time, a scratch on the beak, and said, "Well, I'm thoroughly exhausted now, after that story. If ya'll will excuse me, I need to take a nap. I'm sure the fisherman would love to take the day off and give you a ride home to di island, Chester."

"Ya, no problem, mon!" said the fisherman, happily.

I stood up, and said, "Glad to have you back, Chester. And if you ever disappear again, don't hesitate to not expect me to go looking for you."

"I will, or won't, or something," said Chester. He and the fisherman started to head towards the docks, but he turned, and said, "I almost forgot; Jack is throwing me a welcome home party at the rum factory tomorrow night, if you want to come, Harry."

"I wouldn't miss it for the world," I said. "Just try not to get lost between now and then. No returning wayward sled dogs to their owners in Alaska."

"I wouldn't dream of it," said Chester. "They'd deserve to run away to paradise, too."

"Might need a haircut to enjoy the heat, though," I said. I waved goodbye and shuffled through the sand to my favorite hammock, and sat and spun my way into gravitized, netted heaven. I put my hat on my belly and Starch on top of it, then closed my eyes and nodded off to the sound of swaying palm trees and the nearby ocean.

Everything was right with the world again, at least my small portion of it. Chester, Cosimo, Starch, and I were all where we belonged, especially Cosimo, and I had nothing to do again but recover from whatever the hell it was I'd been doing for the last few days. It was time to relax, and put back on any of the Hemingweight I might have lost in my travels.

Oh Auntie Em, there's no place like home.

Chapter Twenty-Three

"It's those changes in latitudes..."

Jimmy Buffett was singing something on the rum factory stereo system about going off to see the world, which was all well and good if you hadn't already found your one particular harbor. Which I had, although I wasn't in it at the moment. But di island was pretty damned close, and if I hadn't stumbled upon Paradiso Shores, it might have ended up being even more particular than it had.

It was curious that Jack and I had both ended up where we were because of wrecks; his in a snowstorm with a Suburban, and I in my rummy one on the beach. But that's how life treated you; it was full of strange little coincidences and happenings you were better off just going with, or you'd never be able to look back and notice how strange they were to begin with.

Although being where I was at the moment, standing on the patio of a rum factory next to a tropical ocean, had been more of a choice and not a random occurrence. And like almost every other choice we make in life, it hadn't been entirely without its downsides. I still missed my sons, even if they didn't seem to miss me. And I sometimes hankered for the little things that living back in America put right at your fingertips; sports, movies, and a pizza you didn't have to go to a neighboring island to pick up. But there were a lot of things that I didn't miss back in that old life of mine that I'd made walk the plank, as well. And on an evening like tonight, you'd be hard pressed to find a negative thought about life in my noggin.

Di Island Rum Company was simply a great place for a party. To state the obvious first, there was rum, and lots of it. There was so much that you could literally go swimming in it, if you wanted to crawl into one of the fermentation pots. Of course, you might drown, but that was probably better than coming back out and risking the beat down that Jedidiah was liable to give you when Jack sicced him on ya for defiling his rum. But the option was there never the less to turn the tables and swim in liquid gold, instead of having it swim in you.

And then there was the atmosphere. The factory was situated in a little nice old island style building, brightly painted both inside and out in a multitude of hues. But the stone patio next door to it was my favorite spot of all, outside under the sun or stars, on a hill overlooking the ocean. There you had the whole island package; palm tress, weather, music, food, tiki torches, thatched umbrellas, colored lights and lanterns; you name it, it was there for your eyes and Caribbean soul's approval. Ambiance so fine.

And speaking of ambiance of a totally different sort, Chester had broken out his party hat for the occasion. The thing seemed to grow each time I saw it, with a new little umbrella, feather, plastic shark or such stuck into it somewhere. And when you added the lights strung through it, it made Chester's small coconut sized cranium look like a shrine devoted to the worship of just what we were doing; celebrating enjoying the hell out of life.

"Great party, eh?" said Pat, di island's sole resident Canadian, who loved playing the cliched Canuck to the hilt.

"Yeah, it is that," I said, as I squeezed my way past him through the happy sea of people mingling and laughing. "I wonder what they're doing in Minsk right now?"

"Probably the same thing, just with fuzzier hats," said Pat.

I smiled and continued on my way, until I reached my destination at the corner next to the bar.

"I'm not gonna do that again for a while," I said.

"And what that was that?" asked Maggie.

"Pee," I said. "Too far to go."

"Then you're right; you probably won't do it again for a while," said Jack. "Nature of the process. Although it's inevitable, especially when you keep refilling your tank."

217

"I guess it's all good. If we didn't empty out, we'd run out of room to pour more in, and that's the fun part," I said. "Speaking of which, who was watching my drink?"

"Jolly Roger was, but he drank it," said Mags.

"Sorry, mon; I got confused," said Roger. "I'll go get you another."

"Thanks," I said. As Roger departed on his errand of mercy, I saw a wall of denim coming towards us out of the corner of my eye, and instinctively put my hackles in the upright and locked position.

"Hey, Maggie, do you wanna dance?" said Gus, while shuffling around in a poor impersonation of someone with rhythm.

"Sorry, I'm not allowed," said Maggie.

"You're not allowed to dance?" said Gus.

"Not with you," said Maggie.

"Gee, I wonder who made that rule," said Gus.

"I'll be glad to tell you if you're too stupid to figure it out for yourself," I said.

"Harry, I'm hurt," said Gus.

"Probably not badly enough to suit me," I said.

"After all we've just been through together, are you trying to say we're still not friends?" said Gus.

"Yeah, mon; don't be like that," said Jack. "One love, remember?"

"Come on; let's shake on it," said Gus, extending his hand.

I looked at it for a moment, then said, "Alright; I was only kidding, anyway. I guess I don't hate you after all," and I reached out to grab Gus' hand.

And at the last second, Gus pulled it back, and said, "Gotcha!"

I glowered at him for a moment, something I always enjoyed doing, and said, "What I meant to say was I don't hate you as much as I did, which still leaves plenty of room for intense loathing." Then I put my arm possessively around Maggie. "But you're still not good enough to dance with my girl."

"Fine. I'll go find Faith; she's always ready to dance," said Gus.

"You do that," I said. "And try and keep your clothes on tonight."

"No promises," said Gus, and he moved farther out of my personal space, though not far enough since he was a pilot and not an astronaut.

"Seriously, what's so hard about getting along for you two?" said Maggie. "It sounded like you were okay on your trip together, so I know it's possible."

"Possible, but not probable," I said. "It's become like a staring contest now, and neither of us is gonna be the first one to blink."

"So you admit you don't really hate him, don't you?" said Maggie

I sighed. "I suppose he's alright, if you insist."

"And you could just as easily be friends with him, couldn't you?" said Maggie.

I looked at her, and said, "Let's not get carried away here; I'm not ready to be BFF forever with the guy. And if you want to go any farther with this psyche session of yours, you're gonna have to get intimate with me on a couch."

"In your dreams," said Maggie.

"And yes, we could talk about those too, while we're at it," I said.

Little Akiko suddenly came up to me from out of the crowd, stood on her tip toes, then gave me a kiss on the cheek before disappearing back into the throng of people.

"What was that all about?" I said, rubbing my cheek.

"I guess she wanted to thank you," said Jack.

"I didn't really do anything," I said. "Nothing that really helped, anyway. Chester returned himself to di island, in the end."

"At least you tried, though," said Jack.

"Akiko doesn't talk much, does she?" said Maggie.

"Nope; that's one of the things we all like about her," I said.

"Here ya go," said Roger, while handing me a fresh Captain Billy's Black Dog Rum and coke.

"Thanks. This reminds me; where is Black Dog this evening?" I said.

"He's out sailing on the water," said Jack. "Sometimes he'll come to one of these shindigs, but most of the time it's a little too much for him with all the people."

Just then I heard a loud, *"Yee-haw!"* and when I looked to see where it was coming from, found that Gus was standing on the short wall that surrounded the patio, and was in the process of unbuttoning his shirt before ripping it off and whipping it around his head.

"I know just how Billy feels," I said. "At least about *some* of those people."

"Here we go again," said Roger, rolling his eyes.

"I guess he couldn't find Faith," said Jack.

"Avert your gaze, Maggie," I said. "This is something you don't want to see, or you're liable to get turned to stone."

"It's something I don't want to see, or something you don't want me to see?" said Maggie.

"Both," I said.

"Yeah, I'm sure you'd be looking the other way if that was Faith up on the wall stripping naked," said Maggie.

"That's totally different; Faith is Faith, and Gus is very..." I said, and glanced back over at him, immediately wishing I hadn't. "Guslike."

"Well, at risk of being banned from the Rumwreck, I happen to think he's kind of attractive," said Maggie.

I picked my jaw up from off the ground where it had dropped to, and said, "You're kidding, right?"

"No, he's cute, in a Humphrey Bogart kind of way," said Maggie.

"Well, this is liable to be the end of a beautiful friendship," I said.

"You're just jealous," said Maggie.

"Of him? Fat chance. *Mags*," I said.

"Don't call me that," said Maggie.

"You just bought yourself a whole night of Mags-dom, young lady," I said. "If you had a room nearby, I'd send you to it."

"Are you going to forbid me to ever see him too, dad?" said Maggie.

"I just did, remember?" I said. "And I am turning into Papa Hemingway, so behave, *Mags*."

At which point Maggie socked me hard in the arm, spilling my rum all over the both of us.

Finally Gus finished his strip tease, minus very much teasing, jumped off the back of the wall, and went tearing down the beach towards the water. I'd seen him do it before, but this time, no one seemed inclined to join him.

"I tink ol' Gus jumped the gun dis time," said Roger. "Looks like no one else was ready for skinny dipping, yet."

I was about to agree with him, but just then a whoop emanated from the middle of the crowd and Pat pushed his way through, clumsily clambered over the wall, and went running towards the ocean after him, flinging his clothes as he went.

"I don't think that's what Gus had in mind," said Jack, with a chuckle.

"Neither do I," I said. "I'm sure he'll be pleased to no end with his new swimming buddy."

"Is Pat by any chance, you know..." asked Maggie.

"If you mean gay, then no, he's not," I said. "He's Canadian."

"Ah; that explains it, too," said Maggie.

"Wow, man; this is so cool," said Moon Man, as he swayed up to us.

"What is?" I asked.

"All the positive vibrations. Can't you feel it?" said Moon Man. "There's only a few tiny traces of negativity running through this whole crowd."

"The strongest one is probably mine; *Mags* just said that Gus is cute," I said. "And we *all* just saw two slabs of Pat's Canadian bacon go bouncing to the water, and that should account for the rest."

"That would probably do it, yeah," said Moon Man. "Great to have Chester back though, isn't it?"

I looked for Chester's hat bobbing along, and found it and he doing some crazed sort of dance with Akiko, his arms flailing around as if he was drowning. "I wonder what you call that dance? Chester looks like he needs rescuing."

"Maybe it's the Baywatch," suggested Moon Man.

"Now how do you know about Baywatch and none of the other TV shows?" I said.

"Nicole Eggert," said Moon Man, and as we all stared at him, added, "Hey, I'm still a dude, dudes! Although Hasselhoff rocks, too."

The music over the PA suddenly stopped, and an eerie silence fell over the crowd, as if brought on by the mention of the Hasselhoffer. Which was finally broken when Boyd played a lick on his bongos and shouted, "Conga line! Form up on the hat!"

Jedidiah began banging out a rhythm on the steel drums, and people began to arrange themselves into a Belafonte-like queue. I knew from experience that the most important thing to do now was to grab the right hips, which in this case were Maggie's, of course. As long as everyone else did their part, it was all you had to worry about; the rest would sort itself out, so to speak.

Eventually we all managed to form a colorful island snake, winding and bouncing our way between the tables, inside the factory through the rum pots, and back out the door onto the patio again. And all the while led by the Chetster, as if following the guy who'd just been lost for over a week was a really good idea. But perhaps like Rudolph's nose, the hat may have made all the difference in the world.

Things pretty much went downhill after that, meaning the fiesta turned into a whole lot of raucous fun. The conga line went straight into an hour long steel drum and bongos dance, the crowd slowly dwindling as the dancers dropped out and went home. But that was hardly the end, since as usual, a smaller, spin-off bonfire party for the diehards broke out down at Jack's tiki house on the beach. And, as usual, those diehards included me.

When you take someone who used to have to keep their juices flowing in a northern winter and move them down to the tropics, those same twelve volts tended to last forever. And of course, it helps when you're mixing in all that solar power. I ended up stumbling down the beach just before sunrise, passing out in one of the hammocks at the Coconut Motel, next to Monkey Drool's. Which was perfect when I had to do more stumbling the following morning, as in next door to the bar.

Mags told me later that day that she'd been trying to get a rise out of me with all the Gus stuff, but I'm not sure I believed her. There had been something in her eyes when she'd mentioned the Humphrey stuff, but maybe it was more for Bogie than Grizwood. That was my hope, anyway; I'm not sure I could live in a world where Gus and Mags were an item. War, greed, climate change, and I can still manage a smile. But I draw the line at any chance of happiness if there were ever to be a Maggie and Grizwood pairing.

By the time we got home the day after the party, it was almost sundown again. We'd spent the day visiting, snacking, recovering, and visiting some more, making our way from heavenly place to heavenly place. It was always hard saying goodbye to my friends on di island, but like all of our homes, it was nice to get back to my own, quiet, little Shangri-la. And di island wasn't so far away; you could make it out from the shores of Paradiso, if you just used your imagination. Or a strong telescope from the cliffs above the Keyhole.

Besides, I loved my own little archipelago. Yes, it didn't have a pizza place like di island. Or the quaint little shops. Or the seven bars. In fact, it only had one watering hole; mine. But all of the things it didn't have were what I treasured about it. Like Robinson Crusoe and Gilligan, my island's bare essentials belonged to me. There may have been other people living on Paradiso Shores, but the island was mine. In my heart anyway, which was where it mattered most.

I was truly the king of somewhere hot.

Chapter Twenty-Four

"*Di Beach*; dat be di best tropical type movie," said Kian.

"No way; you be forgettin' all about *Di Mighty Quinn*," said Keyon.

"Hey, Di Beach got Leonardo," said Kian.

"Yeah? Well, Di Mighty Quinn has Denzel," said Keyon.

It was the usual morning breakfast debate at the Rumwreck, except that unusually, this time it wasn't *at* the Wreck. Instead, we were having a picnic on the beach inside the Keyhole Cavern, next to the turquoise waters that flowed in from the Atlantic Ocean.

"Has anyone ever noticed that John Candy's character's name in *Summer Rental* is Jack Chester?" said Maggie.

"Interesting point," I said, picking at the last of my mango chicken. "I'll have to tell Captain Crazy and the Danielson about that the next time I see them."

"Are you tryin' to add dat movie to di debate, Maggie?" asked Kian.

"No, because it would be pointless, since all of you would be wrong, anyway," I said.

"Oh yeah? Den what be di very best beachy movie, Harry?" said Keyon.

"Captain Ron, mon," said the fisherman, who I'd thought was asleep, since he'd been leaning back against the wall of the cave with his eye closed for some time.

Kian and Keyon looked crestfallen.

"Di fisherman be right, Keyon; we forgot all about dat one," said Kian. "It not even be close."

"At least Captain Harry didn't get the chance to pick you for a change," said Keyon.

"No, hee-hee; the fisherman gets to win di debate dis time," said the fisherman, with a smile.

"That's what I was gonna say, though," I said. "Captain Ron, that is. And I'm not surprised it's your pick too, fisherman, considering the eye patch and all that."

"I still say we should have left somebody behind to watch di bar," said the fisherman.

"What does that have to do with it?" I said. "And why are you bringing it up again, now?"

"I just wanted to let you know dat just because I agree wit you about di movie, it doesn't mean I tink you're right about anyting else in di world," said the fisherman.

"Look, I told you, you old coot, it doesn't matter if the Wreck is open right now or not," I said. "If someone from Paradiso shows up, they won't care that we're closed; it'll be the old *"No problem, mon"* thing

229

all over again. And if some tourist from a neighboring island drops by, gets pissed off and swears he's never coming back again, so what? Chances are he's never coming back again, anyway, or at least I can always hope that he won't. Besides, don't we all deserve to have a little fun together every once in a while? So shut up, and have fun; now!"

"Another long winded speech from di hairy blow hard fish," said the fisherman.

"But some fun sounds like a good idea to me," said Keyon. "Wanna go for a swim, me brother?"

"Yeah, mon," said Kian, and the two got up and dove into the water.

"If both of you are done arguing, too, do you want to join them?" said Maggie.

"I'm done wastin' my breath on him for now, but I'm gonna snooze, instead," said the fisherman.

"Then I guess the rest of my schedule is free, so let's get wet," I said, and I stood up, and switched from my Captain Harry voice to my bad Captain Ron one. "After all, if anything's gonna happen, it's gonna happen out there."

"I was wondering how long it would take you to try and work a quote in," said Maggie.

"Yeah, it was inevitable," I admitted.

We got into the cool water and splashed lazily around with the twins. Swimming in the Keyhole

Cavern always reminded me of being a kid; not that I'd ever spent much time in caverns or quarries, being way too much of a city boy at the time for my own good. But it brought to mind tales from Mark Twain, and daydreams of being an explorer or pirate. Some places we only see in our heads, but if we're adventurous enough when we're older, we can get to see them first hand. And the Keyhole was definitely one of those kind of places.

I dove under the surface of the clear water and swam up underneath Maggie, doing my finest Jaws impersonation. I picked her up on my shoulders as best I could, but since the water was too deep for me to stand on the bottom, I didn't have much balance, and we toppled back into the brine. I came up laughing, but then noticed that Mags was fiddling with one of her ears.

"Dang it!" she said.

"What's wrong?" I said, worried I might have hurt her in some way.

"Oh, I lost one of my earrings," she said.

"Sorry; I was just-" I began.

"Don't apologize; it's no biggie. It's just a cheap pair of rhinestones," she said.

"I'm glad," I said, relieved.

"That my mother gave me on her deathbed," said Maggie.

"I'll be right back," I said.

It looked like Mags had been about to say something, but I took a deep breath and dove under the water before she could manage. I swam to the bottom, which was roughly ten feet down, and looked around for the earring. I couldn't find anything, and was about to give up, when I spotted something silverish laying on the sandy bottom. I quickly paddled over and grabbed it, but it was a small chain of sorts, and not the earring.

I snagged it and tugged on it anyway, figuring it might be a necklace dropped by one of the many swimmers in the Keyhole. But it ended up being attached to something, which turned out to be an aged looking brass tub. I pulled it out of the sand, quickly looked it over, then swam back up to the surface.

"You didn't need to do that; I was about to say I was just kidding about it being an heirloom," said Maggie. "I bought them on e-bay with a bunch of other jewelry, I think."

"That's good, because I couldn't find it down there, anyway," I said. "But I did find this," I added, holding up my discovery.

"What is it?" said Maggie.

I shrugged. "I don't know; let's go back to shore and find out."

We paddled the short distance back to the beach, and I got out of the water and examined the tube more closely. It was about a ten inches long, two inches in diameter, and heavy for its size. The whole thing was badly corroded, but I could make out ornate etchings in the metal. The silver chain attached to a loop welded near one end, and there was a spot near the opposite one where it looked like another loop had broken off; perhaps the chain had been used to carry it on a belt or something. There was also a cap on one end, also made of brass, held in place by four metal screws.

"We've got to get this thing open!" I said, excitedly.

"Yeah, we do," said Maggie, looking very comely, all wet and beach girl like.

"Hey, fisherman; do you have a screwdriver in your tackle box?" I said, wishing I'd mobilized the Swiss Army this trip.

The fisherman opened his eye, and said, "Yeah, mon; but what did ya break now?"

"Nothing," I said, going over to where his rusty old box sat next to him. I opened it and dug through it, finally finding a regular screwdriver.

"Do you think those screws are going to come out that easily?" said Maggie. "They look like they've been in there forever."

"There's some WD-40 in di box, too," said Keyon, who had come out of the water to see what all the fuss was about.

I leaned down and dug around some more, found the wonder spray, and said, "Got a lot of fish that don't want to come off the hook or something, fisherman?"

"No, but he's got a cranky engine on his skiff," said Kian, joining us, too.

"Ain't dat di truth," said the fisherman, standing up and joining our circle.

I sprayed and pried, twisted and turned, and cussed and swore, all under the expert advice of my ever helpful compadres. I'd managed to take out or break off all but one of the screws (there always has to be one stubborn one) and was about to give up on the last of them and hand it to Mags, the island grease monkette, when it finally gave way and moved under my last ditch effort.

I frantically turned down the home stretch, my wrist yelling at me to stop exerting it before it really got sore with me, and then suddenly the screw fell unceremoniously to my feet in the sand. I grasped the end cap, and was surprised to find it was already loose, perhaps from the half a can of WD-40 I'd sprayed on its couplings. I pulled it off and handed it to Mags, then looked inside the tube.

"What's in dere?" said Kian, his eyes as big as a kid's on Christmas morning.

"A piece of leather," I said.

"Dat's it?" said the fisherman.

"What did you expect, a gold brick?" I said. I stuck my finger inside and gingerly pulled the rolled up leather out. Then I dropped the tube and went over to Maggie's picnic basket, knelt down in the sand, and rolled the parchment out on the top as everyone gathered around me again.

"Holy crap," said Maggie.

"Dat be an understatement," said Keyon.

"Is dat what I tink it is?" said Kian.

"If you be tinkin' it's a map, then yeah, I tink that's what it be," I said.

"Holy crap," said the fisherman.

"Yeah, we all agree on that," I said.

"What do you think it leads to?" said Maggie.

"I have no idea," I said. "But you can bet your buttocks I'm gonna find out; it can't be any harder than finding Chester."

"You didn't find him; he found you," said Maggie.

"Details, details," I said. "All I know is that maybe now I have another mystery to solve. And maybe we can try to unravel this one together."

"Maybe we can at that," said Maggie.

And maybe I'll have something else to write about on my new old typewriter, after all.

But not before this son of di beach squeezes in another nap or two.

The End

From The Author

While the story you've just finished is the first in a new series of books, and was written to be able to be read on its own, it features many of the characters from my previous Island Song Series novels. If you enjoyed it and wish to go back and read all five of the stories, their order is as follows. Mahalo!

Di Island Song Series
I'm Gonna Live My Life Like A Jimmy Buffett Song
Jack And Di Rum Song
Let Di Song Of Change Blow Over My Head
I Just Had To Go Back To Di Island

The Captain Harry Series
Captain Harry, The Son Of Di Beach
And The Mystery Of Crazy Chester